The
*I*diot *D*ance

The
I diot *D* ance

A NOVEL

ERIC FROST-BARNES

Contents

Twelve chapters, Nine months, and One life.
(Well, sort of . . .)

~ for Raleigh ~
"The Scoob"

~ for Kate ~
"Beauty"

That old cat is so confused
That old cat is so confused
Been beaten, brought down,
left all bruised
Said that old cat is so confused

—Folk Song

A P R I L

ONE

Sex and the Single Schmuck

INDIANA JONES IS THE VERY ESSENCE OF MAN. He is strong, intelligent, good with a rope, and always ready to throw his well-lit, celluloid ass on the line. I, Terry McGuire, am not the very essence of man. I am somewhere adrift between manhood and childhood, either not ready—or not willing—to make the leap out of one and land permanently into the other. According to my closest female friend Drea, I am floating in "man-boy limbo."

"Guys who are edging toward thirty should not have posters of Indiana Jones hanging in their bedrooms," she explains in a tone that reminds me of Ms. Hoffman, my fifth grade teacher, who no doubt would agree with Drea's opinion.

My bedroom, like the rest of my apartment, is decorated sparsely in a style that only a financially—and emotionally—struggling, single, twenty-nine year old bachelor could appreciate. A twin bed rests in one corner, with my boom box beside it serving as the room's stereo system. Against the far wall is an old dresser with various colognes and change scattered on top, and an ever—growing pile of laundry next to it on the floor. Pairs of old Vans and Doc Marten boots lay in one corner, with a couple greasy ball caps in another. As for décor, two framed posters hang on opposite walls, facing one another in a permanent stare down: Indiana Jones—Harrison Ford to the lay person—squared off against L.A. Laker extraordinare Kobe Bryant, Kobe forever captured in one of a thousand acrobatic dunks. The posters, a real source of pride for me, let whoever enters my lair know that sports and movies are vital to keeping this particular man-boy happy.

Drea, however, does not approve of the room's current look, nor does she seem concerned with my feelings, especially where my framed posters are concerned.

"Of course *Raiders of the Lost Ark* is a cool movie," Drea says as we look at the perfectly pressed poster, the glass frame keeping it safe from any possible harm, minus a serious earthquake. "Steven Spielberg's directing ability isn't what's in question here. It's your interior decorating skills that *need* a severe overhaul."

I know better, but ask anyway. "What's wrong with Indiana Jones on my wall?"

Drea glances at me, her large dark eyes giving me a look of pity, as if she is staring at a condemned man, or in my case, a condemned man-boy.

"What?" I ask, a nervous smile coming over my face. "What's that look for?"

Drea turns back to Harrison Ford once more as she explains, "You've got to understand, Terry, that when girls in their twenties go out with guys nearing thirty, the girls want to see a hint of . . . *progression.* A girl wants to know that the guy she's seeing is actually moving in a direction. Is he in a good job? Is he capable of taking care of himself? Does he have a decent apartment? Or is he still at home with mom and dad? And does he still survive on money from his parents?" Drea turns to me and pats my cheek for effect. "We like guys who are self sufficient, sweetie. They don't have to be driving around in a brand new Mercedes, but they do have to have *their* name on the registration—not mom's. They've got to want a better life for themselves."

"So what does—"

"Uh!" Drea stops me before I can start. "A guy's apartment is an extension of how he's doing in the real world, and I don't mean that crap on MTV." Drea then gestures to Indiana Jones. "And when a girl sees posters of Indiana Jones and some basketball player, certain warnings are going to go off in her head."

"But Kobe Bryant's a—" Again, I am shut down, Drea holding two fingers to my mouth.

"Uh-uh. Keep it zipped. You asked me what I thought of your apartment and I'm giving you an honest answer."

I look at my waif—like friend; deeply regretting I opened my mouth in the first place. "Yes," I sigh. "You are."

Drea gives me a phony smile, and moves to the Kobe poster. Honesty. A quality that for the most part has died out with the California Condor, except in that uncommon person who would rather tell it like it is than worry about what people think, good or bad. Drea Smith is that rare person. At no more than five and a half feet and maybe a hundred and ten pounds, Drea is a Mack Truck of a personality, rarely hesitating to share what she thinks, and always willing to slug it out with the brashest of them. Bright as hell, Drea, at times, comes off like a human firecracker, full of life and spark, but is equally capable of knowing when to tone it down, if her opinions will do nothing more than hurt feelings. Cruel is one thing Drea Smith isn't. Tell it like it is and fear nothing. Always walk with equal amounts of compassion and honesty, and compromise for no one. Welcome to the primary set of rules on Planet Drea.

"Okay, enough with the posters. Look at this wimpy little bed of yours! Any sensible girl's going to fear she's in her old high school boyfriend's room." Drea moves to my bed and stands on it. Apparently, *any* regard for my feelings is on hold as she continues her style assault. "This bed is insulting. All a tiny bed like this says is that you're the kind of guy who, after a bit of the 'Ol' bump and grind,' wants the girl to leave so you can spread out on your puny mattress for one. You've got to have a king or a queen size at least! Something that says, 'Hey, you beautiful woman, I want you to stay the whole night. I want you to make yourself comfortable in my home. I want to bring you breakfast in bed, as a token of appreciation for shagging my lights out the night before.' Then, you can slide the tray to the side and go at it again, without worrying about knocking plates to the floor. Why? Because there's *room* for it. And these sheets! For God's sake, burn 'em and head for the nearest Stroud's."

For a moment I just stare at my fiery friend. Her short, platinum blonde hair is whiter than the wall and ceiling behind her, her bangs stopping just above her eyes. I glance at the bed for a moment, and turn to Kobe, pointing to the poster's bottom left corner.

"You know he signed this just for me," I tell her. "Right there, says my name and everything. That's Kobe's handwriting! You know he's already got a couple championship rings, right?"

Drea bounces up and down on my bed as she talks. My eyes catch a flash of her milky white belly as her baby doll T-shirt rises and falls. "You can either keep Kobe and remain trapped in man-boy limbo, or you can buy a Dali or a LaRoche, something that doesn't cry out 'I'm still sixteen,' and replace these juvenile posters, inching yourself that much closer to manhood. It's up to you, sweetie. I'm only here to help."

As I watch this twenty-six year old semi-working actress bounce, I can't help but wonder if she really is the final authority in the maturing process. Or Feng Shui.

"So you broke it off with Janet, huh?" Drea asks as she continues the bouncing.

Christ, she's gonna start in on how to re-do your single life now . . .

"Yeah, well, it seemed like the only thing to do," I say in a way that sounds like I'm trying to convince myself. Her question has come out of left field so I hedge before saying more, wanting to sound like I know what I'm saying. "She just wasn't, I don't know, my type."

I just shrug and watch Drea on my bed. Drea's breasts look great beneath her T-shirt, the way they rise and fall, the way her stomach—

"She was too together for you?" Her words about Janet slap me across the face as all concentration is forced back into my foolish reality. The word "together" hangs in the air; thick and heavy, full of sub-text.

O-kay, here we go . . .

I glance up at Drea's face, at the goofy smile she's sporting, and give her a look. "No, she wasn't *too together* for me. She just wasn't . . ." Another pause, with me now trying to remember what I didn't like about Janet.

Don't even start, McGuire. Get back to decorating the bedroom, it's safer.

I look at Kobe and then pivot back to our original, less turbulent topic.

"If I get a bigger bed, can I keep Kobe and Indiana on the walls?"

LOOKING AROUND SCOTT Janwankowski's apartment, Scotty J to his friends (Even someone with a degree in linguistics could dislocate his or her tongue saying Janwankowski too many times), I feel a little better. Scotty's place is more like a rec room than an apartment. A card table stands where many folks would have a dining room table. When it comes to card games, Scotty J is an avid player, and a deck of cards is always ready; waiting to be shuffled, dealt, and held. In his living room, in addition to a beat up (but ridiculously comfortable) couch and a fifty inch TV, Scotty has an old fashioned arcade game of Missile Command set up in the corner, the constant flashing of simulated play tempting you over for a quarter free game. Assessing my surroundings, I wonder how Drea would rate Scotty's apartment, were he stupid enough to ask her advice?

"So she brutalized your place, huh?" Scotty asks me as he lies lazily on the couch, a Coors Light in his hand.

Sitting on one of his barstools, I nod in shame. "Brutal is right! She even told me to stash the *Playboys* that are on the back of the toilet. She said girls don't wanna feel like they have to compete with airbrushing."

"Did you tell her you got the *Playboys* for the articles, not the babes?"

I sip my own beer, a Bass, and nod. "She didn't buy it."

Scotty smiles, glances at the Laker-Denver game on TV. "They never do. So why was she scoping out your place anyway?"

I take a long swallow of Bass before explaining. "Remember the other night, I took Janet out? When we got to my pad, I noticed she was kinda checking it out, almost like she was rating it or something. I showed off my autographed Kobe poster, you know, proud of it and all, and she's looking at it like some kinda booger on the wall. And she's not the *first* girl I've brought back where I felt like they were less than impressed with my living quarters. So I asked Drea what she thought, you know, hoping to get a woman's opinion. Someone who doesn't have anything at stake."

There's a knock at the door.

"It's open," Scotty calls out.

Isaiah, carrying a six pack of beer, walks in. He instantly moves to the TV and asks, "Is it still close?" Isaiah's long frame towers over the large television, one of his thick, dark hands resting atop it, as his eyes focus on the screen, on the game before us.

"Lakers up by five, halfway through the third," Scotty informs him.

Setting the beer down, Isaiah shakes hands with both of us, then turns his eyes back to the game. "So what's up, my pale brothers?"

"Terry's apartment is immature," Scotty pipes up. "Least, that's what Drea told him."

"She didn't say it was *immature*, she just thinks it could use a little more . . . okay, she thinks it looks like a high school guy's bedroom." I take another long, slow drink.

Isaiah smiles, knowing. "It *is* like a high school guy's place. But that's what makes it perfect for you."

"What about Scotty, here?" I fire back, pointing to the arcade game. "This place is a fucking Chuck E. Cheese!"

Scotty J, missing the comment, mumbles something about ordering a pizza, his eyes locked on the game.

Opening a beer, Isaiah takes a drink and gives me a look. Suddenly, his dark eyes light up. "You and Drea didn't sleep together, did you?"

"You ask me this almost every time! No, we didn't have sex. Drea and I are friends. *Friends*. No different then you and me, or me and Scotty J," I tell Isaiah, knowing I'm wasting my breath with him. "The only difference between you clowns and her, is that she's good looking."

"That's not the *only* difference," Scotty J mumbles before sipping his brew.

Isaiah glances at the TV and yells at Shaq to make his free throws. "I'm telling you, she digs you. Always has, always will. You guys are as close as brother and sister."

"Exactly!" I say. "The key words being *brother and sister*. And since we're not from West Virginia, nothing's coming of it."

Scotty explodes with a booming "yeah" as Kobe finishes off a two-handed slam.

"You guys wanna get food? A pizza? Some wings?" Isaiah asks.

"I'm going to head out after the game. Got to work on the column." I say, and then ask, "We're all still on for a run in the morning, right?"

"Sure," Scotty replies.

"Twice around, right?" Isaiah asks, sounding motivated.

I nod a yes. All three of us sit quietly for a moment, our collective focus on the game and drinking beer.

Isaiah then turns his attention to me, an odd grin creeping onto his face. "So tell us *why* you called it quits with Janet?"

Scotty sits up, the game momentarily muted. "Oh, man, you didn't? You idiot, she was perfect!"

"That's the problem," Isaiah adds. "She was *too* perfect for Terry, here. Not fucked up enough, am I right?"

I look at my two nosey friends, their eyes hungry for pathetic excuses and bullshit reasoning.

I've got to start keeping more things to myself.

"YOU KNOW, TERRY, golf's a great way to meet nice ladies," My Pop tells me, as though the thought of a woman dressed like Arnold Palmer is an attractive one. "Most of 'em have steady, good paying jobs. Not like some of those flaky actress—types you tell me about."

If you're interested in topics like Augusta, Titanium Drivers, or the Golden Bear, then my father, Mike McGuire, is your man. If you need counseling on a wayward relationship, or an inspirational speech on why you should continue your writing career, better seek guidance elsewhere. Pop, God bless him, has become, over the course of nine years, the kind of avid golfer who in any other circumstance would be diagnosed as obsessive to the nth degree. And for his only son, whose writing career is fledging on a good day, Pop believes that helping him run his Pro Shop up in Monterey is the *only* answer that makes sense.

"You know you turn thirty in December?" he asks in a way that comes off more like an accusation than a question.

"That's weird," I begin, letting the smart-ass in me come out. "I had a birthday last year in December . . ."

Pop doesn't miss a beat. "How many people you know in their thirties, who are still chasing a pipe dream?"

"In Los Angeles? About three *million.*" I reply, now ready to get off the phone. "And thank you, Pop, for considering my writing ability a—"

"You know what I mean, Terry." he says in that way only a parent can. "You're a good writer, and you know I believe that. But the odds of anyone making a long term, successful career of writing are about as likely as me winning the Masters."

Very few things, profound or otherwise, can escape Pop's mouth without him encompassing a reference to golf.

"Pop, things are just a little lean right now, that's all. I'm still writing the column, and I'm bouncing around a few ideas for a script I wanna do."

"What do they pay you for that sex stuff?" The way he asks tells me that no monetary figure will please him.

Say three grand an issue, see if he even hears you.

I decide to try honesty (Drea would be proud). "It's a monthly column, and the magazine pays me six-fifty for each article. Pop, it's a good magazine, you know this. They've even run articles on your favorite topic a few times."

"Yeah, that's true. Can't be all bad, right?" he concedes, and then proceeds directly to the big question. "You want me to send you a couple hundred?"

The temptation is there, but then I remember Drea's comment about guys living on their folk's money, her point valid—and irritating. For a second my mind weighs the choices. "If you wanna send me fifty, I'll buy some groceries. But I can pick up some extra dough working at my friend's video store."

There's a pause on the other end, then, "You sure? I don't mind sending more. I want you to eat something other than that Ramen garbage you like so much."

"Thanks, I'm cool. I'll call Todd tomorrow, see if he can work me into his schedule this week. I'll be okay." Despite wanting to ask for more, I feel fairly good about my decision. Maybe this moves me a hair closer to manhood. Maybe.

"I know you'll be okay," he tells me. "I want you to move forward, that's all. I want you to be happy. To feel good about things. You've had it hard enough as it is."

"I know. We all have, Pop." I say, then decide to end on a different subject. "How's Tricia?"

Pop's tone lightens at the mention of my little sister. "Tricia's good. She's out with some guy right now, studying. She's keeping the grades up real nice. You ought to call her. She'd like hearing from you. Know that you're still alive."

"I'll do it this week." I say, glad to hear him pleased with how sis is doing. "I'm going to go, gotta get some writing done."

"All right." Again, there's a pause before Pop speaks up. "You know, I've got a close friend over at *Golf Digest*. Maybe he could pull a few strings, get you on as a staff writer. At least, maybe get you some free-lancing."

Thickheaded parents of the world unite.

WHEN IT COMES to writing, many of us go through certain rituals before getting down to the actual work. Some writers, in the tradition of Hemingway, will pour themselves a drink (or four). Others will do everything from putting on background music, to meditating, to playing computer games until they're good and relaxed. One well-respected Hollywood screenwriter even admits to masturbating before she ever picks up a pen or turns on her computer.

Me? I stare into my aquarium, looking over the red and green rocks, the small plants, their green leaves lightly moving in the smallest of currents created by the filter, its soft humming one of the more relaxing man made sounds. For reasons I can't explain, watching that tiny, eight and a half gallon world allows me to momentarily forget about my own. After a minute or two, I'll grab one bottle of water and either a Bass or Guinness, and head for my desk in the dining room, which according to Drea, is where a dining room table should be ("You can't serve Greek salad to your date when there's a computer in the way!"). Once my beverages are in place—and any other unforeseen distractions are dealt with—and the computer is warming up, I head for the stereo and pour over the choices. If you're a writer like me, who always works to music, then the perfect selection is essential. Say you're writing something romantic. Al Green is good, as is Roxy Music (anything by Bryan Ferry), or the soundtrack to *Somewhere In Time*. If you're working on something fairly lighthearted, R.E.M. and early Pretenders are always winners, not to mention John Lee Hooker, The Police and Miles Davis (Miles for when lyrics are jamming you up creatively). Just like knowing what works and what doesn't in sex, being aware of what gets you "in the writing mood" takes practice and precision. Of course, that doesn't mean that what you write won't be complete bullshit.

My column, "Sex and the Single Schmuck" was born of the realization that, at the tender age of twenty-seven, I didn't know a goddamn thing about the opposite sex. Sure, I'd been around the block a few dozen times, but the truth is I was becoming increasingly confused as to what women wanted, and worse, how to give it to them. After a handful of free lancing successes in *Spin*, *Maxim* and *Esquire*, I landed a regular column in an L.A. monthly called *Angelino Style*, where for the past year I had droned out twenty-five hundred words a month on topics ranging from foreplay to having to buy breakfast. At six hundred and fifty dollars an article, I secretly prayed I hadn't reached the pinnacle of my success, but the money was nice and since my apartment was ridiculously cheap (praise Allah for rent control), I could actually pay my rent and utilities. Odd jobs and the occasional humbling month at Todd's video store were what kept me from drowning financially.

Half a Guinness down and I start in on the June column. The subject is the good people of L. A. and their fascination with Las Vegas, and the endless parade of sin and vices that little oasis provides. While I'm outlining the notes, my mind drifts back to my old man and our conversation. To a certain degree, I know what he was saying is right. Here I am coming up on three decades of life, and half the time I'm working in a video store asking middle-aged perverts if they want their pornos in a bag. Not to mention the job requires wearing a goddamned nametag. I have a theory that if you're still wearing a nametag as a thirty-year-old in the workforce; you've really screwed up somewhere along your employment journey.

I turn back to stare at the aquarium, a soft white light coming out. The Talking Heads are singing "Road To Nowhere" in the background when I decide to write my grandma a letter instead of starting the column. Grandma Kate, my mom's mom, always knows what to say, and how to get through the toughest of times with a genuine sense of dignity and hope. It's an art I have yet to grasp.

Maybe a letter to her and I'll be able to shake off the doubt and get back to work.

At the very least, writing Grandma Kate and sending her my love should be good for my karma.

THE HOLLYWOOD RESERVOIR is three point two miles of scenic beauty that *almost* makes you forget that just around the corner looms one of the largest, most heavily polluted cities on Earth. Only when running across Mulholland Dam, at the first mile mark, can you see downtown L.A. below, the dozens of skyscrapers jutting upward into a gray haze of too many cars, machines and people. The rest of the time squirrels, cotton-tailed rabbits, birds, and the occasional snake mix in warmly with tall pines and bottle-brush trees, giving the paved run a semi trail-like feel.

Isaiah, Scotty and I run at a decent pace even though none of us got much rest the night before and all of us drank at least a little. While I was writing my grandma, Isaiah had been on a date with Sherry, a buxom brunette with a perfect bubble butt and great long legs. Scotty J was also out, he and another friend scowling the different clubs, both getting some phone numbers, neither going home with company. As we run, Scotty continues to lobby for why Isaiah and I should consider using the Internet for meeting women.

"You'd be surprised," he says. "I've gotten laid a dozen times out of it. These girls are just like regular women."

"Thing is, Scotty," I begin, my breathing fairly hard as we round another corner of the course. "There's something kind of . . . *desperate* about looking for dates through your computer."

"And hanging out in bars hoping to get a phone number isn't desperate?" Scotty asks, a shade too defensively.

"Now wait a minute. You were hanging out last night, looking to—"

Scotty, his own breath coming quicker as he interrupts Isaiah. "I *am* desperate! But the fact is, the more shit you throw at the wall, the better the chances that something sticks."

I glance at Isaiah, then turn to our boy. "That's a nice theory, there Scotty. You ought to embroider that on your pillows at home. Show 'em to first dates."

Scotty gives me a look when Isaiah hits my arm lightly. "Oh man, look at this girl coming our way."

Scotty J and I glance up and see this leggy girl running toward us. She's maybe in her mid-twenties, and possesses the kind of body that belongs in the Smithsonian. As she passes us by, she offers a little smile to no one in particular (probably because we look like *The Three Stooges*, the way we're all bright-eyed and gawking at her). Her face is tan, with nice wide eyes, and her long dark hair is pulled back into a ponytail. After passing us, Isaiah, Scotty and I all look back in perfect unison, all with our own thoughts, none of which could be that different from the others.

"That girl is death," I say to them. "Did you see her face?"

"I couldn't get my eyes off her tits!" Scotty expresses, with his usual Cary Grant like charm.

"Gorgeous. Abso-fucking-lutely gorgeous!" Isaiah announces, smacking my arm again. "You better get her phone number, her name at the minimum."

I look at him. "Me? What're you, kidding?"

"She was looking at *you*, McGuire! I know you saw her do it." He says this with enough conviction that now I'm not sure he's simply blowing smoke up my ass.

"Uh, uh. She was just glancing over at *us*. All of us, cause we were so obviously smitten, checking her out." I say back, then steal a last glance before the jogging vision disappears around the corner.

"She was looking at you. That smile was for you!" Isaiah continues, shaking his head at me in disgust.

I look back one last time, seeing only the pavement and the

fence that borders the woods. "No, that wasn't at me. She looked over to acknowledge us, that's all. You know, the way runners do, like they're letting you know that they're goddamned tired too, and to just finish strong." My bullshit meter moving off the charts, I decide to shut up.

Having never been good at approaching girls I didn't know (no matter how beautiful), I wasn't about to start by stalking some poor woman on a fairly desolate running course. She could scream, or worse, be carrying mace.

Isaiah looks at me, again with the head shaking. "You better take Scotty up on his Internet offer. Skittish mother fucker."

AFTER OUR RUN and a quick breakfast, I clean up and head for Video Schmideo, the video store my friend Todd co-owns and manages. Todd Smalley, easily one of the nicest people in Los Angeles, is the kind of guy who looks out for anyone he deems worthy, and as luck has it, I am one of the fortunate. Having bonded over a mutual admiration for Spike Lee, Todd would, whenever I came in for a rental, tear my ear for a good twenty minutes about what was new, what was good, and what was nauseating (Todd's word), but worth watching anyway for the sheer twisted pleasure of it. A devoted John Waters fan, Todd and I found additional common ground in movies like *Cry-Baby*, *Pink Flamingos* and *Hairspray*, Todd constantly remarking about the late great Divine paving the way for so many "limp-wristed transvestites." You see, Todd is not only a movie fan to the nth degree, he's also effeminate enough to make Harvey Fierstein come off like Sly Stallone in the macho department—a feat not easily accomplished.

I walk into Video Schmideo and Todd greets me immediately. He obviously sees something in my body language, and saves me an ounce of employment—begging self respect by proclaiming how Cory, this skinny drama queen, just up and quit, and how I have to do him a "major favor" by helping out with a few weeks work. If I were gay, I'd marry Todd in a nanosecond. Instead, I greet him with a handshake, a hug and a deeply sincere thank you.

"Oh Terry, don't worry about it," Todd says, tossing me a set of keys for closing. "It's my pleasure, finally having someone around with some (raising his voice for the other co-workers to hear) fucking taste in movies!"

And like that I am employed. My friend has come through for me, saving me from the ranks of the destitute with a simple read of my starving artist face. Looking at Todd, full of appreciation, I break, and do offer to marry him. It's probably not how Indiana Jones would handle it, but what the hell does he know anyway?

TWO

That Sinister Urge

I SIT ON MY KITCHEN COUNTER, TERRIBLY HUNGOVER, reading the L.A. Times. I read about some poor bastard found dead in the Hollywood Hills. The man's body was found up on Mulholland Boulevard, a hundred yards west of Outpost road, nude and very beat up. The medical examiner's report was not complete, but early reports said the man, who was white and in his late twenties, had been stabbed multiple times in his abdomen, upper thighs and genitals. Police theorized that the victim, his name being withheld until his family had been notified, was what they call a "dump job," that he had been murdered elsewhere and his body left on Mulholland like an empty six pack of soda. The article about the dead man goes on to say that there were no witnesses (of course), and that the body had been found early yesterday morning by an older woman out walking her dog.

My head throbbing, I move to the fridge and take a long drink of orange juice. I think about Mina, this little red-haired vixen I dated for a couple of months, and how she loved to have sex against my car at the various observation points on Mulholland and the PCH. For a few seconds I wonder if there was more to her interest in that particular road than I thought. Maybe she used it as both an aphrodisiac *and* a dumpsite for ex-boyfriends. I shake off the thought; figuring paranoia is getting the better of me.

After another swallow of juice, I head for the bathroom, grab a few aspirin and pop 'em down. Looking in the mirror, I see the hickeys on my neck and upper chest, their color a deep purple, almost black. A quick shower, and I'll be half my old self, I hope, give or take a dozen love bruises from the night before.

Last night had gone well. My date with Sabrina started out with an early casual dinner at Swinger's on Beverly Boulevard. From there we hit Oliver Stone's latest movie out in Century City, had a drink at Houston's afterwards, and then started going at it while waiting for the valet to bring around my Cherokee. Deciding a few more drinks were in order, we drove out to Sunset, headed over to Red Rocks, and drank enough Tanqueray Tonics to make Ted Kennedy proud. Back at Sabrina's apartment, we never made it past her living room floor, our limbs entwined, our lips together like both of us were in dire need of oxygen. Hands working overtime, with most of our clothes thrown to the side, Sabrina started in on my neck like Bela Lugosi. Normally, I try to avoid hickeys (they're cute when you're thirteen, cheesy and juvenile for anyone old enough to vote), but I was smashed and whatever Sabrina's technique, it felt really good. A moment later Sabrina got up and came back with a pair of handcuffs dangling from one finger, a sexy little smile on her face. Now this is one area where men and women tend to differ. Many women, even caught up in the mood, might become apprehensive or suspect of any man who brings something as constricting as handcuffs into the sexual mix. Guys, however, see rope, cuffs, whatever, and their eyes light up like a golden retriever spotting a pig's ear. Anyway, once the cuffs were on and my bound hands were well over my head, Sabrina continued her vampire impression, her mouth moving further and further down my body, leaving a broken path of fresh beauty marks.

Out of the shower, my headache has now improved to a dull thud. I look in the mirror again; the hickeys are still standing out far more than I hoped. Fun last night, irritating to leave this morning looking like a domestic abuse victim. I grab my hairbrush, and realize that working at the video store tonight will be hell; half of the gay clientele will see me as some kind of S&M prince. Not to mention that until the hickeys fade completely, it will be nearly impossible to date anyone else.

Sabrina and I are anything but a couple, yet every few weeks or so we'll go out, have a good time socially, and either sleep together or not. Drea says this phenomenon is known as the "fuck buddy" agreement. According to Drea, having a fuck buddy is terrific, except that no matter how mutual the terms, one person will inevitably begin to either grow too close, or begin to pull away, leaving the other person confused, hurt, or most likely both. So far Sabrina and I seem to be on the same level (except in our love of hickeys), neither wanting more from the other, but both really enjoying the perks of our arrangement.

I feel a sharp pain in my upper back as I pull on my pants. I figure that being shackled and worked over like I was probably has earned me a trip to Isaiah, my friend and friendly chiropractor. Hopefully, he won't give me too much static about the hickeys, my hangover already beating me down enough. Hopefully, he'll take a little pity and show an ounce or two of mercy. Knowing Isaiah like I do, I don't hold my breath.

ISAIAH TUGS AT the T-shirt I wear, looking beneath it, a smile on his face as he spots a few more of the hickeys. "Looks like you got into a fight with someone with very small fists," he says, moving to sit on the corner of his desk. "At least I know you're having sex every now and then."

I sit on the adjustment table and glance at one of the charts hanging in his office, the chart showing the human skeletal system. "Actually, we didn't have sex last night. Not biblically, anyway."

"What'da'ya mean, you *didn't* have sex?" Isaiah stands, and walks to a college style mini-refrigerator beside some file cabinets in the opposite corner. He opens it and looks at me. "How does anyone who's twenty-nine get so many hickeys, and *not* get laid?" Isaiah grabs two Cokes, tosses me one and heads back to his desk, giving me a bewildered look as he sits.

"She handcuffed me and instantly became this relentless sucking machine," I say, shrugging. "Remember that old *Star Trek*, where Captain Kirk's people are getting knocked off by those green salt-sucker thingies? They had those suction cup mouths and hands? That was Sabrina."

Isaiah gestures to my neck, at some of the bruises. "You gotta tell her to knock that shit off, Terry. Nothing wrong with having some oral love, but come on! You realize you haven't got a prayer of even getting a date from any other woman looking like that?"

I glance at another chart, this one of the muscular system and nod knowingly, "Uh, yeah, the thought crossed my mind."

Isaiah sips his soda, sets it down. Clapping his hands together, he walks over to me and puts his hands on the base of my neck, feeling around. "Let's see what damage you and the hickey monster have done. Sit up and relax your shoulders."

While Isaiah assesses the damage, my eyes comb over his office, the various charts showing degenerative disks and vertebrae, and the differing sections of spinal curvature. In another corner, hanging off the ceiling, is an overly green and thoroughly fake fern (Isaiah, tired of replacing the real plants, had accepted that his medical expertise didn't extend into the art of Horticulture).

"The pain is a little lower, between my shoulder bla—"

"Shut up and let me do my thing," he grumbles. "You sound nervous, like half my white clients. They afraid to let a black man keep his hands around their throat for too long. Think I might still resent 'em for my great granddaddy's oppression."

"I had nothing to do with that," I pipe up in true smart-assed fashion. "You know I'm down with the cause. That I saw *Malcolm X* twice."

"Take it easy, 'White Chocolate,'" he says, his hands now moving around in preparation for the big adjustment. "Or I'm liable to give you an extra crack."

A few minutes later my back feels a hundred percent better. My headache and hickeys are all that remain from my liaison with Sabrina. Looking around the office, glancing at the adjusting table, I cannot resist asking, "You ever use this thing with any women?"

"You mean, have I ever done the nasty in my place of work? Where my career is on the line? My reputation?"

I sip my Coke and nod yes.

Isaiah walks to his table, glancing at it as though thinking of some specific memory, then eyes me in mock suspicion. "You wearing a wire for the medical board?"

I step toward him and arch my back, "Please speak clearly into my right nipple."

Isaiah laughs, nods. "I've had a couple of women on this thing. Was fun, too. You wanna use it for your column?"

"Maybe," I start, "if I'm desperate for material."

A SLUG OF Joe, on Sunset near Book Soup, is one of those newly discovered coffee houses where the semi-famous will grab a quick Latte or Mocha and the wannabe famous will hang out each afternoon hoping to move up to the level of the semi-famous. Andrea "Drea" Smith, tough girl extraordinare, labors here five days a week, when she's not working on the occasional commercial or day-player part of the latest WB teen-show. Serving coffee and keeping her ears and eyes wide open, Drea eavesdrops for any tidbit of information which might help her get closer to the world of the working actress—or actor, as she calls herself. Drea has had her share of opportunity, landing national spots for Taco Hut, MCI and McCabe's Lite (a lousy beer that claims to be made from the freshest water in the Appalachians—something I'm not sure they should be boasting about). She just has yet to nab the *one* job that'll put her over the top, both career and money wise. Truth is, Drea could easily live for six months off the money she makes on these commercials, rather than slaving away at the coffee house. Instead, she puts good chunks of her earnings away for rainy Mondays and indulging in the occasional vacation. So here she is, working for nine bucks an hour as an assistant manager—dealing with the endless attitudes of those who think they're on their way— slinging coffee like some high school grad who never planned further ahead than her next kegger party.

Having twenty minutes to kill before I'm wanted at the video store, I drop in to see Drea and grab an iced Mocha. She doesn't notice me, so I slink up to the counter, lean in closely behind her and whisper, "I'll take a coffee and *you* to go, you fine thang."

Drea turns around smiling and leans into me, our faces an

inch apart. "Well the coffee's three bucks and very hot. But me, I'm priceless and far too heated for your tame self."

The two of us are grinning like fools. I step back and fan myself in jest, "I think my testicles finally dropped."

Drea grabs a paper cup and heads toward the machines. "See," she starts in, "you *are* moving closer to manhood. You want your usual?"

"Please," I reply, glancing around the outside patio area where twenty or so young trendy types enjoy the early summer afternoon and their respective drinks, among them Val Kilmer and this incredible blonde, her hair in pigtails. "The 'Ice Man's' out there."

Drea looks at me, unsure.

"Val Kilmer, in *Top Gun*? His character's name was 'Ice Man.'"

Drea glances outside, makes a funny face, "I've tried to wipe the entire 'eighties' out of my mind." She moves closer to me, her eyes on my neck. "Somebody's got a hickey!"

I shake my head, wishing it were cool enough for a turtleneck. "Somebody's got a *dozen* hickeys."

A huge, goofy smile washes over Drea's face, her eyes lighting up. "You either went out with that Sabrina, or you've started dating Ike Turner."

"The former, thank you. They're that obvious?"

Drea passes me my iced coffee, then touches one of the hickeys lightly, "Sweetie, if they were neon, they'd be less noticeable."

Knowing I'm going to fight off endless comments tonight from Todd and all the boys at the video store, I sigh dramatically, wishing I'd stayed in last night, or at least kept a muzzle on Sabrina.

"So listen," Drea starts in, "I'm getting my apartment painted this Friday. Care if I crash for the night on your couch? I don't wanna breathe in too many fumes, start seeing pink elephants." Drea sips my coffee, nods, "This's good! I should give myself a raise."

I look at my friend, at her deep, dark eyes, and her little nose, the way it turns up just a bit. How could I deny someone so cute? "Mi casa, su casa. Let me know when you want the house key."

Drea leans over the counter and kisses me on the cheek, "You're the best. It'll only be the one night, so you don't need to give me keys."

I sip my coffee; the cool liquid feels good on my throat. "I'd rather give 'em to you. Then I'm not pinned down by your coming and going."

Drea wipes the counter and nods at an incoming customer, an older man with sunglasses and a beret. "Thanks, Terry. You'll be home after work?"

I nod, "Yup. Give me a call." As I head for the door, I look back at her, "You sure my place isn't too immature for you?"

Drea smiles, while pouring an iced tea for the man in the hat. "I'll deal. Maybe I'll bring decorating mags with me. See what we can salvage."

I SIT ON a folding chair at Scotty J's. He and I, along with another friend of ours, Pete, are waiting for Isaiah to arrive, making this Poker Game's foursome complete.

Drea had an idea for my bedroom; on how to give it a more "mature" feel, yet still keep the playfulness I was so obviously attached to. Going over her concept, Drea spotted the small bottle of lotion peeking out from under my bed, my hands instantly claming as she bent down to pick up the white bottle. Giving me a knowing smile, Drea handed the lotion over and whispered it was better she found it than some close-minded first date.

Finishing my story of the morning's cruelty and Drea's handling of it, Scotty shakes his head and sips his Coors Light.

"Did you tell her the lotion's for dry skin?" he asks.

I nod, glancing at him and Pete, "I said I sleep with the window open. That the night air dries my skin out. Something weak like that."

"And she bought it?" Pete asks, maybe thinking he can use this particular excuse for himself down the road.

"Not a chance," I tell him. "She looked at me like my nose had grown a foot."

Scotty J laughs, "They always do. As men, we need a better excuse than dry skin. No chick falls for that one."

Pete and I swig our beers, while Scotty pulls out a cigar from his shirt pocket and lights it up.

There's knock at the door. Scotty calls out that it's open. Isaiah enters, carrying a bag of salt and vinegar chips and a six pack of beer. Trading hellos and what's-ups, Isaiah sits down, after a brief pit stop in the kitchen. Now that we're a quartet, we all converge on the table, ready to play the card game of champions—or at least bad poker players—Five-Card Stud.

Scotty looks at the beer Isaiah is drinking, turns to Pete, and finally to me. "All of you brought your own beer. I've got plenty of—"

"No one likes that piss you drink, Scotty," Isaiah tells him. "Besides, you're lett'n us play cards in your home. You're the host. As guests, we're supposed bring something over with us, as a gesture of appreciation."

Pete nods in agreement as I look at my back—cracking friend, "That was nicely put, Isaiah. You sounded like Martha Stewart."

Isaiah thanks me, squeezes my shoulder. "So what's been going on, gentlemen?"

Scott Janwankowski, ever ready to blurt out the embarrassing confessions of others, pipes up in his deep voice, "Drea caught Terry whacking off this morning!"

Pete laughs in surprise as I lower my head, irritated. Isaiah looks at me, a smile on his face.

"Don't listen to moron over there," I say, gesturing at Scotty as he puffs proudly on his eight-dollar stogie. "All that happened was she came over and found a bottle of hand lotion by my bed."

"You say it was for dry skin?"

I nod, "Didn't fly."

Isaiah shrugs, "Never does. So what kinda lotion was it?"

"What the hell kind of question is that?" Scotty asks.

Isaiah sips his beer before answering, looking patiently at our Polish friend. "Doesn't surprise me you don't get my question. When it comes to jerking off, there's a real science to making it a pleasurable experience. To gett'n the most out of it."

Sounding more and more like an African-American male Dr. Ruth, Isaiah continues his thoughts on the subject of whipping your skippy, with Pete, Scott and I all ears. "Think about it. You don't use just any magazine or porno; you *choose* the right one. The one that'll let your mind really get into it. The same should go for your lubricant. You're not gonna grab a bar of soap after taking time to perfect the visual aspect of the experience. You need to create the right feeling while jerkin' a soda, pulling your pud, waxing the dolphin. The right accessory, the right *aid*, in what is meant to be pleasurable. Something that adds to the mood."

For a moment "The Great One" is silent, we peons only staring at him in awe.

Scotty, his mouth agape, begins the Q&A portion of the lecture, "Did you learn all that in Chiropractic School?"

A COUPLE HOURS later (and fifteen bucks poorer) Isaiah and I walk together toward our cars. For several strides neither of us say anything. After a minute of enjoying the night air, Isaiah turns to me and says with conviction. "Next time, my brother, try vegetable oil. I know it sounds freaky, but trust me, it works like no other."

I look at him, unsure, wondering if he's playing me. We begin walking again, neither of us speaking up, each of us with our own private thoughts.

Vegetable oil? Hmm . . .

ONE OF THE many misjudgments heterosexual guys make about homosexual men is that they are physically weak. If you are straight, and someone calls you a "faggot" or a "homo," you instantly feel your manhood being attacked; your ability to do what is one of the most primal male acts is suddenly in question; the ability to fight back. The ability to prove you are a MAN. If you are gay, then there's no way you can fight with limp wrists. Any guy that participates in anal sex or even kisses another man is a pansy by nature; this golden rule beaten over our hetero-inclined heads from an early, impressionable age. Words like pussy, wimp or fag all generally have the same effect on young men, and if you don't fight back with either harsher words or fisticuffs, then the label sticks like a scarlet letter, and you quickly become a punching bag for whichever grade-school bully gets to you first.

So now, standing behind the counter of Video Schmideo, where three-quarters of the customers are gay, I can't help but admit to myself that probably ninety percent of these "pansies" could beat the hell out of me without even messing up their hair. Gay men like to date men who are in shape; therefore they too will hit the gym, pool, or plastic surgeon in order to look as good as the men they seek. And by nature (at least according to my friend Todd), gay men are not as lazy as straight men. From how to dress to how they work out, gay men have those sensible/motivated genes that seem to have escaped most straight guys.

This guy that exits with *Swoon* and *There's Something About Mary* is no taller than me, but probably outweighs me by twenty pounds in good old fashion muscle. The funny thing is, if I looked even half as cut as he did, I could probably date twice as much, not to mention, have a hell of a lot more energy, both in bed and in the outside world.

Todd, catching me looking at this last customer's body, leans in and waves a hand in front of my face, "Snap out of it, Terry! Don't move to the Dark Side. Your bony ass wouldn't have a chance!"

I laugh at his comments, shaking my head. "I wasn't checking him out, but I will say—"

"Oh, God, I was!" Todd exclaims, looking through the plate-glass window as the customer walks off in front of it. "His name's Chris. Always rents at least one comedy."

"I was thinking I gotta start working out. Seeing all these guys in ridiculously good shape is making me feel more insecure than usual," I say.

"Don't you run a lot?"

I nod, "Yeah, I'm in shape, kind of. I'm just not in *shape*. I wanna start trying to run competitively. Maybe if I lift some weights, I'll improve my times, race wise. At least I'll feel better looking in the mirror. I think."

"All runners are skinny, though. Look at those crazy guys that do marathons. None of them weigh more than Kate Moss," Todd says, his point a good one. "If you're going to keep running and you want to bulk up, you're going to have to start eating like the fat guy that explodes in *Monty Python's Meaning Of Life*. All you'll do is eat, eat, eat. Unless you get yourself a trainer who can show you some tricks of the trade. 'Cept, something tells me that's not affordable right now." Todd pokes me in the stomach, and moves to help two girls as they reach the counter, movies in hand.

The very next guy I help dwarfs Arnold Schwarzenegger in size, the tank top this mountain wears advertising Gold's Gym. He hands me his movie, and I see that he is renting *Mildred Pierce.* An image of this guy at home eating six chicken pot pies while zoning on Joan Crawford instantly pops into my head. Seeing that this man's bicep is the size of my head, I wanna drop and do a dozen push-ups just to try and make myself feel better. Either that, or say fuck it and take up smoking again.

What we choose to believe as children, in the name of fear and ignorance, is ridiculous. Some of us as adults. I decide these thoughts should end up in a future column of mine, that maybe there's something to what I'm thinking about.

That, or I've watched *Torch Song Trilogy* once too often while working here.

THE DAY BEFORE Drea stays over, she takes me to Trader Joe's and Ralph's to do a little shopping. This is yet another fundamental difference between the sexes. When a guy says he's got to do a little shopping, he means a quart of milk and some peanut butter, or one pair of shoes. A "little shopping" for a woman is a minimum of two or three stores, and at least that many full bags of the stuff they've just bought. One ex-girlfriend used to buy new shoes every week, apparently to go with the other weekly household items one needs to subsist (bread, water, toilet paper) on.

So here we are, in aisle eight of Ralph's, with Drea filling the grocery cart as though Y2K were a monthly threat. According to my spunky, baby-doll tee-shirt wearing friend, another drawback to my apartment is the constant state of emptiness of the kitchen cabinets, food wise. This fact telling prospective girlfriends I'm only interested in feeding myself, and that I'm not even capable of doing that.

"I know you're magical when it comes to Mac n' Cheese, but most girls wouldn't mind a Merlot, or the occasional Chinese Chicken Salad," she tells me while dropping a can of white pepper into our cart.

"What am I gonna do with white pepper?" I ask, gazing at the canister, befuddled. "What *is* white pepper?"

Drea tosses in two boxes of sugar; one brown and one white (perhaps she's in the mood to bake a cake or pie). "You need white pepper, Terry. You can't dump black pepper on everything!"

I give her a suspicious glance and ask, "You're racist when it comes to pepper, aren't you? You've got a problem with Afro-American pepper."

"Cute. Very cute," she says and moves for another item.

In the next aisle, Drea drops in a few different types of healthy soups as I guide our cart with precision, not allowing myself to step on the lines dividing the floor tiles.

"You're only staying one night, right?" I ask, now unsure.

"Relax. Some of this is for my own place, too. I'll drop it off before the painters get started. Hopefully, they won't paint my cupboards shut," she says. "But you *are* letting me get you a few things." Apparently, the word few in Drea's personal dictionary means twenty to thirty. "Do you need any oils? Canola, or vegetable?"

As she asks this question, Isaiah's face springs into my brain, his expression lit up by a bright toothy grin as he tells me the wonders of masturbating with vegetable oil. "Trust me, it works like no other." Those words echo through my head as I eye the golden plastic bottles, the name Wesson jumping off the shelf at me.

I grab a small bottle and hold it in my hand for a moment. Maybe I should get a second one, I think to myself, not necessarily wanting to use the same oil for cooking chicken as I do for choking the chicken.

"You need two bottles?" Drea asks, seeing both.

"Um, one's for my neighbor. I borrowed some from her and forgot to give it back," I lie, tapping my head in forgetfulness for effect, as though Drea were catching on to the fact that her twenty-nine year old friend was considering using goddamned veggie oil like KY-Jelly.

You're going to live to regret this, McGuire . . .

As we continue down the aisle I glance back, worried that somewhere Isaiah is waiting, watching me with Allen Funt and a hidden camera.

AT THE APARTMENT, Drea helps me put away the so-called few groceries, looking on with pride at the now half full shelves.

"At least now it looks like somebody eats here once in a while," she says, ruffling my hair. "I gotta get going. I'm hitting an audition for some play over in West L.A. This little forty-seat theatre."

A heavy knock at the door. Drea and I look at each other.

"It's your place sweetie. I'm not expecting anyone," she says.

I head for the door and open it to see Isaiah standing there, a small paper bag in his hand.

"What's going on?" he asks and walks in, spotting Drea. "Hey, girl!"

Isaiah enters the kitchen and sets the bag on the counter. He and Drea give each other a warm hug.

"Finally, I get to see you again," he tells her. "Like the pants. Very nice."

"I was going to swing by your office last week, have you adjust me. Maybe take you for lunch," Drea tells him. "But I got called in to the coffee house. We all need to go out, have a few drinks together."

Isaiah smiles, "You name the time and place and I'll buy the first few rounds."

Drea slugs his arm, liking the attitude, "Sounds great." She then picks up the bag Isaiah brought with him, and opens it. "What'd you bring Terry?"

Isaiah gives me a funny look as she asks the question. My own eyes widen as I see her pull the all too familiar shaped bottle from the bag.

"Vegetable oil?" Drea asks, then turns to me. "How much of this stuff do you need?"

Sister, you have no idea . . .

For a moment (though it feels like an hour) nothing is said by either Isaiah or me; Drea's eyes move back and forth between us.

"I . . . I borrowed Terry's and thought I should bring him a replacement."

Good, at least Isaiah is making an effort to not completely jam up the situation. As the words leave his mouth, his eyes widen at me, as though giving me a cue to finish his thought.

"That's, uh, why . . . why I had to borrow my neighbor's oil," I explain, slower than I'd have liked. "Cause this knucklehead skated off with mine. He's always doing that, borrowing vegetable oil, butter, hairspray."

Looking at Isaiah's short, tightly kinked hair, I figure toothpaste might've been a better choice than hairspray. I turn to Drea and give her a weak smile. "So tell us about this audition."

Drea glances at the clock on my microwave, "Shit, I gotta get going! I'm gonna be late."

I reach into a drawer in the kitchen and find my spare house key attached to a bottle opener. "Bring whatever you need over tomorrow. If I'm not here, make sure you lock up when you go."

I hand the key to Drea as Isaiah makes another attempt to distance us from the vegetable oil, "I heard you and Terry are having a sleepover. You kids have fun."

Drea smiles, heads for the door, "Thanks Terry. I'll see you two later."

"Break a leg at the audition. Not really, but you know what I mean," I tell her.

"Make Terry sleep on the couch tomorrow. Don't let him keep his bed!" Isaiah calls out to her.

Drea nods in agreement, and then mumbles something about my puny mattress and exits.

Once the door is shut, I pull out the other two bottles of Wesson. I hold them together for my dopey friend to see. Isaiah shrugs, as if to say, "I didn't know."

"We buy a few more bottles, we could hold women's wrestling here," he says, stacking the third bottle atop the other two, forming a mini culinary cum lubricating pyramid.

MY NIGHT HAD been spent writing, trying to make my deadline and to get back into the swing of things. For every day that I don't write enough—or not at all—I can feel myself growing crankier, and becoming more consumed with my growing insecurity about how seriously I take myself as a writer. Looking at ninety-nine percent of everything I have ever written, I know that I'm a competent writer at best. But I also know that the more I write, the better I'll become, this realization adding to my frustration whenever I find myself slacking off. The odds are so incredibly stacked against me making it as a successful writer anyway; I feel that if I don't bust my ass for at least a few hours a day—the way a professional athlete would train daily—I will see my craft (and any talent) quickly stagnate.

Whenever I am writing, in contrast to music serving as mood and background, all other possible interruptions are dealt with. A note is systematically taped to the front door reading: "Am WRITING. If you bother me, I will BEAT you senseless with my KEYBOARD!!!" The ringer on my phone is turned off, my voice-mail catching all would be callers.

Once I finish with my column's first draft, I use the toilet, grab another bottle of water and check for any messages.

Sabrina's sexy voice is on the line, asking if my hickeys have faded (they have, mostly; the bruises now a light ugly yellow), and if I want to grab dinner next week.

Drea is next, telling me she thought the audition went well and that she'd be over sometime in the early afternoon to drop off her stuff for the night, before heading to the coffee house. She also hoped the writing was going well for me (Drea being one of the few acting types who didn't drone on endlessly about their career or craft).

Isaiah is the last call, busting my chops about how my computer was probably collecting dust while I whacked off like a madman to my new stash of veggie oil. "Be sure you use a healthy amount," his recorded voice advises. "You don't wanna chafe."

Standing there with the phone in my hand, I cannot help but think my friend is way too concerned with my own love life. Or complete lack thereof.

IT IS NOW three a.m. and I have just finished the final draft of my column, and frankly, I'm feeling pretty good about where it's at.

Cha-ching! That'll be another six hundred and fifty bucks, please.

I know how little money that is, but I still feel good making it. I place the printed copy in a large envelope, along with a note to the editor, saying hello. Standing and stretching, I move to my phone, and check the messages again. The truth is my sex life is rather mellow right now (minus Sabrina, the twenty-something vampire), but I still dial my access code in hopes an old flame or someone I met recently and traded numbers with has decided that not only do they need a man at this late hour, that that man is *me*.

The computerized female voice tells me I have no messages at this time. Not surprised a bit, I still feel slightly bummed as I hang up. Oh well, if I can't celebrate the completion of my column with anyone, I'll just take in some late night TV and eat a plate of Kraft Mac n' Cheese, the meal of the damned and lonely.

LUCIDITY IS SOMETHING my dreams don't usually contain, the current one being no exception. I stand in an empty kitchen, my parent's voices barely audible from someplace I cannot see. Though I'm able to make out my pop's voice, my mom's seems more fuzzy, more distant, as if barely there. In front of me is an open doorway, which I walk through, hoping my folks will be on the other side of it.

I stand in some brush, with several trees—oaks, pines, and palms—all around me. No longer able to hear my mom or pop, I turn back for the doorway and trip over something. A man's body, bloated and pale, lies face down naked in the brush. My hands are wet as I scramble to get away from this corpse, my brain warning me not to look at *why* they are wet. My legs are wobbly and give out beneath me. As I look back I see the dead man roll over and sit up, his lifeless eyes aimed at mine, his lips black and puffy as he speaks.

"Don't sweat it, Terry," he says in a manner that reminds me of every game show host I've ever seen on TV. Pine needles and leaves stick to his chest. Several small wounds mark the dead guy's neck and shoulders, a couple of them opening a bit further as he speaks. "Long as you keep dumping them bitches like garbage, you'll be A-O-kay! But remember, do your part to help control the pet population. Get yourself neutered as soon as possible . . ."

I crawl away as fast as I can and stop only after I find myself in aisle eight of my local Trader Joe's. Standing in the middle of the aisle is my most recent ex, Janet. She holds a single glowing bottle of Wesson in one hand, gives me a wave, and then briefly flashes me her breasts. And then, with a wink and a smile, she turns and walks out of the aisle, the white floor beneath me growing brighter, until I have to shut my eyes.

When I do wake up, I glance around my room for what can't be more than a few seconds, making sure no dead guys or glowing bottles are nearby. I feel my eyes closing and slip back into sleep, my mind already moving onto the next picture show.

BECAUSE IT WAS nearly four-thirty when I finally flopped into bed, I didn't bother to set the alarm, leaving my waking up to fate and the noise production of my neighbors. Rolling over, with my eyes squinting at the ridiculous amount of sunlight in the room, I try to focus on my clock. Ten minutes to one . . . in the *afternoon*. I try to remember the dream I had, then sit up and mull over how cool it is to start my day about five hours later than the average L.A. citizen (not counting musicians and prostitutes). Knowing I've already met my *Angelino Style* deadline and still have a couple hours to kill until I need to deliver the article to the magazine's offices (I don't use fax machines or the Internet; my way of rebelling against the newer forms of technology), I stand up and go over my options. I could run the reservoir and clean out my lungs, maybe see that stunningly beautiful jogger from the other day. I could also go over my column one more time, in case the late hour affected my eyes. A few corrections may still be needed. Or I could spend the next hour in a far more responsible manner; wanking off.

When it comes to masturbating, most guys—gay or straight—will feel that sinister urge come on without any real motivation. Sure, seeing someone incredibly attractive is big, as is a certain erotic memory popping into your mind, but the awful truth is no legitimate reason is needed. In the shower and you suddenly feel like soaping your rope? Have at it. Wake up early to find a penile tent pitched in your bed? Knock 'em dead. Besides, isn't simply *having* a penis enough of a reason?

So here I am at one in the afternoon, my living room blinds still drawn, the TV and VCR ready with a seventy-minute porn called *Video Vixens, Volume 29* playing quietly, and me running around in a towel and the old socks I slept in. I exit the kitchen carrying one of the unopened bottles of Wesson (one of them was already used on some Parmesan noodles, as opposed to my own noodle), and head for the bathroom, wanting to grab a smaller towel for cleanup. In the bathroom, I can barely hear the porn playing—*was that a knock?*—where a young woman's voice is pleading with me the viewer to call her on her very own, very private, nine-hundred line at only six ninety-five a minute. I hear something else as the next porn teaser comes on—*a key working the door?*—but then only hear another woman, this one telling me how hot she's getting just talking about oral sex. I head into the living room, armed with my Wesson, another bottle of lotion (in case Isaiah's full of shit) and my towel . . .

Drea is standing by my television, watching the screen with amusement. With a pillow, a backpack and another small duffel tucked under her arms, she turns to catch me frozen in the hallway, my near nakedness and my jerking paraphernalia in full view. Her eyes bug out like Marty Feldman's as the situation dawns on her. Unable to hold back, multiple snorts of laughter escape her, and in an instant, my entire sexual urge is completely gone.

Vanished.

Erased.

Drea's eyes fall on my socks, then slowly pan up to the towel wrapped around my mid-section, and finally come to rest on what we shoppers call pure vegetable oil.

"I hope that's not the bottle you're giving your neighbor," she says, concerned.

THREE

Six Inches and Dairy Products

NEWSSTANDS ARE GREAT. THEIR PRESENCE is one of the truest signs you live in a big city. The first day after I moved to Los Angeles I headed straight to the newsstand at the corner of Fairfax and Melrose and browsed for a good half-hour, taking in all the sounds, sights and smells of the street. In some strange way, this simple task christened my arrival.

Sometimes, when I feel the need for validation, I'll go to the newsstand on Sunset, near Drea's work, and flip through the different magazines. I always finish with *Angelino Style*, sneaking a peak at my column and the cheesy little photo of me beside my name. Lame as it may be, this ritual consistently brightens my mood. On occasion, a stranger or person I've recently met will place my face and say they've checked out the column, most responding favorably.

Angelino Style hits the market for the upcoming month one week before the current month's end; the May issue still on the shelves when I grab a copy. My article on "the death of the sexual taboo" faces up at me. A slight smile creeps onto my mug as I read a random paragraph. I close the mag, glance around as if someone were watching and head past Book Soup toward A Slug Of Joe.

Drea sits on the counter, talking trash with one of her co-workers, Ben, a nice looking guy with jet-black spiked hair and a pierced eyebrow. Ben and I nod hellos as Drea turns around to see me, a grin coming over her face (I pray she's not picturing me in a towel and socks).

"Hey you!" she says, leaning forward and planting one on my cheek. "What brings you into our little caffeinated world?"

I shrug, "Not much. Felt the need for some coffee, thought I'd say hi."

"Your timing's great. I'm two minutes into a break," she tells me, scooting off the counter. "Grab a table outside. Lemme get a cigarette and I'll bring you a coffee. You want your regular?"

"Please."

"You want *Wesson* with that?"

Looking at my friend, at the dopey smile on her face, I realize last Friday's scenario is not an easily forgotten one. Christ, I feel like a jackass.

"HIS COCK IS sooo big, it's like having sex with a baseball bat!" Drea informs me, her volume a little louder than I'd have preferred. "I feel like I'm going through some sorta reverse labor every time we shag."

We sit outside among the actors and actresses, most working on coffee or tea and cigarettes as they jaw with friends. The sun, though blocked out by a giant canopy, feels good, the air comfortably warm.

The words that have just left Drea's mouth seem to hang in the air; a couple of guys glance over at us. Drea inhales deeply on her cig and looks at them. One guy quickly turns away, while the other gives her a cheesy, flirtations grin.

"Oh, go away! Shoo." she says to this stranger, using her free hand to dismiss him before turning back to me. "I don't know what to do."

"Do you like this guy?" I ask.

"I'm *sleeping* with him! Sweetie, girls shag guys because they do like them. As opposed to guys, who'll shag the hell out of any girl just cause she's still breathing. Anyway, yes I do . . . like him.

He's sweet, smart, funny. He's just got this huge (Drea holds her hands almost a foot apart for emphasis) penis and I'm not sure my body'll last much longer if I keep up this activity!"

This is where the guy/girl best friend thing comes in handy; the following kind of question could never be asked had we slept together at some point. "Don't laugh," I start, "but what about lubricant—"

"I love you to death, Terry, but I've seen what *you* use for lube. Cooking products and my vagina don't mix. Next question."

"O-kay. What about telling him to take it slower? You know, kind of work into it?" I feel like a retarded Sex-Ed teacher as I speak.

Drea sips my coffee, then mashes her cigarette out in the ashtray. "I'm one hundred and eight pounds. There's only so much 'working' before I start feeling like I'm being split-stacked."

Ah, leave it to Drea to take a "PG" conversation and hurtle it toward an "NC-17" rating.

"I always thought women prefer a larger, you know, to a smaller one," I say, trying to keep my voice low. "That size matters?"

"Of course size matters! Why do you think I'm in pain here?" Drea fires at me, hostile. Again, a few people look at us, either curious or annoyed as Drea continues. "It's like that saying from *The Three Bears*, 'This one's just right.' Well, the one I'm bumping and grinding with is not just right. Girls like the guy to have something bigger than a golf pencil, but trying to maneuver a Louisville Slugger isn't any better."

Drea glances inside, and slowly stands, "I should get back in there. I think my ten's over."

I look at her, shrugging, "At least you're moving all right."

"Yeah, well, I'm crying on the inside." Drea gives me a wave, heads for the door. "I'll talk to you later."

I watch the traffic for a moment, thinking, and enjoying my iced Mocha. Did I hear Drea use the words "golf pencil" to describe a guy's shortcomings? I glance inside the coffee house, thinking about my friend and wonder if she's been talking to my old man.

WEDNESDAY NIGHT. CHAVEZ Ravine. Dodger Stadium. L.A.

versus those damned San Francisco Giants. Stopping at the booth to pay for parking, Scotty is handed an application for a Visa Card with the Dodgers' colors on it, the application entirely in Spanish. Scotty looks the app over, more than a hint of confusion in his eyes. I take it from him and tell him to forget it, that even if it was in English, he couldn't afford the interest anyway.

We reach our seats, Scotty, Isaiah and I, second row of the Loge, right in front of third base. Isaiah mentions that we're in prime foul-ball territory. It's the middle of the first, and someone nearby is listening to the game on a portable radio; Vin Scully's voice filling the air. Each of us holds a beer (Scotty the only one excited that it's Coors Light) and a hotdog, my dog between some relish and mustard for company. The commonly held belief about bad beer and hotdogs tasting better at a sports event is one of the strangest and most accurate observations a person can cling to in a world of uncertainty.

Settling in, we talk about how the Lakers are doing in the playoffs, a cutie Isaiah adjusted at work that afternoon, and my upcoming evening with Sabrina tomorrow night. Isaiah reminds me to keep control of the hickey factor.

Halfway through my dog, I recall Drea telling me about her current sexual situation, and wonder how many other men have ever considered their own penile dimensions. Not that I'm worried about having a mini-schlong, but I also never had a woman tell me to stop, that my sidekick was too big.

"Terry? Whatever happened to that one girl, Stacy, the one you brought to Dublin's on Valentine's Day?" Scotty asks, distracting me from my thoughts.

"Yeah, she was cute," Isaiah adds, tipping back his beer. "I almost forgot about her."

"Head case," I say, remembering how Stacy would call two, three times a day, after the two of us had only dated for a couple weeks. Stacy was a sweetie, with great breasts (full and real, as rare as rain in Los Angeles) who liked to laugh. But she was a struggling actress who did a hell of a lot more struggling than acting. This meant she had too much time to dedicate to other things, me being one of them.

Isaiah looks at me, the last of his dog stuffed into his mouth. "She was crazy?"

"She wasn't *crazy*. She just wanted to hang out too much, too soon," I explain. "Kinda like she was into me more than she was supposed to be, you know, that early on. I felt the space thing happening."

Scotty nods, says, "Oh, the space thing, again." He laughs to himself, and sips his beer, his hotdog as yet untouched.

Eric Karros clocks a fast ball hard into the right corner, and rushes to second base. Everyone bolts to their feet, cheering. Isaiah gives the guy behind him a high-five.

The "space" thing for me is a neurotic belief that early in a relationship, unless both people are absolutely lusting for one another, neither person should rush into anything heavy. By heavy I don't mean sex (sex can occur in the first ten minutes of a relationship, if it feels right), but the behavior that often comes from somebody a little too zealous in the dating department.

Space can be maintained by following these simple rules:

#1. Don't start leaving, on accident or on purpose, items of yours behind at the other person's place. Toothbrushes, T-shirts, sunglasses, whatever. None of these things belong anywhere but your own place until at least a month into the relationship.

#2. When calling the person, don't leave painfully long or mushy messages on his or her answering machines or voice-mail before the end of the first month. And don't call he or she more than once a day, unless you have plans and you're trying to firm them up. Then, and only then, can you call a second time. If you need to know why multiple callings are bad early on, rent the movie *Swingers* and fast froward about an hour into the flick.

#3. For chrissakes, avoid using the L-word in the first month to six weeks (again, unless both of you are out of your minds for each other). Telling someone you love him or her is meant to be a special, vulnerable moment. If someone *needs* to hear it, or you *need* to say that you love him or her, this is what shrinks would call co-dependency (as in, not a good thing). This "love" rule is the biggie, and few things are more awkward than an early, pre-mature declaration of love. It just makes everything real . . . messy.

#4. Lastly, don't do anything that could come off as stalker-type behavior. In this day and age, too many people carry firearms and mace. If you're unsure as to what this behavior is, chances are you've already practiced it.

Okay, back to the game . . . .

The Dodgers leave Karros stranded (of course) when some new guy pops up a fly ball, which is caught by the Giant's catcher ten feet in front of home plate, thus ending the inning.

"Too bad she didn't know your rules," says Scotty, watching as the Dodgers take the field. "Maybe with the next girl you bone, you could provide her with some kind of handbook in advance."

"Show her a pie chart or something," Isaiah adds, he and Scotty sharing a laugh.

With Scotty's untouched hotdog making me hungry for another one, my mind wanders back to Drea and her dilemma with Mr. Big Dick.

"Either of you guys ever have a girl tell you your schlong was too big? You know, like it wasn't fitting right?" The words escape me before I realize what I'm asking.

Scotty, who had finally taken a bite, nearly chokes. "What the hell's wrong with you? I'm eating!"

"That's Scott's way of ducking the question," Isaiah says.

"No, that's my way of not think'n about dicks while eating a hotdog."

A heavy-set woman with a bag of peanuts turns around to look at us, apparently needing a visual to go with the conversation she's hearing from the row behind her.

Isaiah looks at me, nudges my shoulder. "You know what torque is? Torsion?"

I sip my beer, trying to remember anything from high-school physics. "I think so," I say. "Something to do with exertion of forces, with twisting—"

"Exactly!" He says. "The force created from the twisting or turning of an object. Like a dick. But this is where *width* counts, not length so much."

Scotty, ready for another bite of his dog, looks at us, irritated. "Can I eat this in peace? Pu-leeeze?"

The crowd at Dodger Stadium cheers with the strikeout of the Giant's First Basemen. Isaiah continues his thought.

"So yeah, having a big dick is a good thing, but not essential."

I look at him, my back to home plate for a moment, "You're not answering my question, Isaiah. Has a girl ever told you, your schlong was too—"

"Only during anal sex."

Scotty stands up, his face contorted. "Come on, you guys! We're watching fucking baseball here! We're not talking about big dicks, or little dicks. We're not talking about tight asses or torque, or whatever the hell you call it. Let's watch the fucking game!"

Before either Isaiah or I can respond, the heavy-set woman leans back to me, speaking quietly, with her eyes on Scotty J.

"Your friend's a little defensive about this stuff."

THE AVERAGE LENGTH of an erect penis is six inches. Funny how we, as a society, put so much emphasis on something no bigger than many household items. A ballpoint pen is close to six inches. A checkbook is around six inches in length. Hell, a goddamned Hostess Twinkie is nearly six inches. Six inches is not very much, it only being, well . . . *six inches.*

This is what most men (and women, for that matter) have to work with. God help us all . . .

FUCK-BUDDIES. WHILE thousands of men and women sweat their upcoming dates tonight, I can just sit back and relax. While hundreds of men rush around buying roses and lilies, I can get away with a cheap bottle of wine, or nothing at all if I'm feeling particularly lazy. Why? Because Sabrina and I are simply good friends who happen to like each other's bodies. No awkward first kiss. No uncomfortable silences during dinner. And no weird feelings if the other doesn't call every three hours just to say hi. Just good old fashioned sexual deviance among friends, also known as fuck-buddies.

Sabrina and I decide over the phone to grab a couple videos, and order in some food. Sabrina says she'll take care of it, that I should head over around eight, and to dress casually.

It is an odd phenomenon, going out with a non-date, knowing that your chances of getting laid are as good as the L.A. Dodgers blowing their pennant race. A shower, for instance, takes on a whole new meaning. Instead of a quickie, the soap connecting with maybe thirty percent of your body (pits, crotch, face, hopefully not in that order if using a washrag), you actually begin taking your time, making sure everything, including the old willy, hacky-sack and back alley get a solid wash and rinse, not wanting your partner finding herself faced with a difficult decision.

While I'm drying off, I glance at the toilet, more specifically, at the *Playboys* on the back of it. Suddenly, that sinister urge is there, maybe to fire off a round before the actual invasion, giving my little friend and me more staying power. Then I come up with a better idea: maybe I should measure the little guy, remind myself that I'm in the top fifty percentile, that six inches is for the masses, not for a guy like me.

When I was a senior in high school, my then-girlfriend at and I had taken a ruler to my better half. The result was a solid seven and a half inches. When she told me the length, I felt like an Olympian. Maybe I hadn't won the gold, but by God, I was coming home a medallist. My seven and a half inches were proof that I, Terry McGuire was a M-A-N, hear me roar.

A few minutes pass with the magazine and my thoughts. My schlong and I now stare one another in the face. I grab the measuring tape, which is ready for this precise moment, when my love-pump is at full force. Stretching the tape from the base to the—

Six and a half inches?

What the hell? Somebody call Oliver Stone, or Agent Moulder over at the *X-Files*, cause something is inexplicably wrong with this situation!

Another go with the tape produces the same results: I am now a pinky fingernail above average. To the naked eye (or a naked woman) my phallus must seem devastatingly average. Typical. Mentioning the extra half-inch now would only create pity, suspicion maybe that I was trying to squeeze out more length in vain.

How did my ex and I get it wrong by a full inch? Did my penis shrink, like an old guy after eighty years of gravity on his spine? Or had my ex, who I think was the one holding the tape, have it closer to my balls, her positioning off by the sheer silliness of our act?

All I know is now I'm an average guy in the worst way. No woman—not Drea, not anyone—would ever complain about my manhood being too large or too manly. I stand there, naked and shrinking, realizing why no woman had ever complained about it being too large in—the—first—place.

All I can do is get dressed and head on over to Sabrina's. Just me and my incredibly boring schlong, although now the word schlong seems inappropriate for my meager means.

Maybe I'm not holding the measuring tape right. Maybe I should try it one more time . . .

SABRINA AND I share a bottle of Merlot, each on our second glass. *Guys and Dolls* plays on the TV, Brando and Sinatra cutting a rug. We watch a few more seconds, then Sabrina tops off both our glasses, the bottle finished.

Sabrina is dressed in worn Levi's and an old Jane's Addiction T-shirt, with her long dark hair piled loosely on top of her head. I find myself glad to be here, glad to be hanging out with my friend. My fuck-buddy. Sabrina, a music consultant for movies (easily one of the coolest jobs in the world) looks her thirty-three years, only the years suit her in a very honest way, as though proof that she has lived life on her terms, with a minimum of compromises made.

"Are you getting hungry?" She asks, sipping her wine.

I nod, "Yeah, but if you're not, I can hold out a little longer. I'll just catch a buzz by the end of this glass."

"I like the sound of that. You are ready, though, to eat a little *something*?"

"Sure."

An odd, somewhat sinister smile creeps across Sabrina's tan face, her eyes lighting up as she stands. "Don't move, young man. I'll be right back."

I watch her leave the room, and then I have a long, slow sip of red wine.

Onscreen, Brando's Sky Masterson eyes lovely lady Jean Simmons, his body language giving him away.

From the bedroom comes Sabrina's voice. "Close your eyes, Terry."

I take another sip and do as I'm told, curious about what she's up to.

"Are they closed?"

"Yeah."

"You sure?"

"Um, pretty sure," I call out, now wanting to open them. "What're you—"

Sabrina's hand covers my eyes, her skin soft. "I want you to relax, babe. I'm going to blindfold you, lead you to another room."

My heart begins to beat considerably faster, fear not being the reason. "Long as I don't wake up missing a kidney."

A soft, cool cloth-*silk?*—is tied around my head, the light of the TV gone. "Luck Be a Lady Tonight" is all I hear for a few seconds, and then Sabrina takes my hand and helps me up, telling me to leave my wine, that she'll get me something else to drink.

"Where are we going?" I ask, excited and nervous.

Sabrina, not in the mood to give any specifics, kisses my cheek. "We're going to play a game."

Taking baby steps toward my unknown destination while Sabrina lightly kisses my ear, I can not help but think Sky Masterson is right about the luck thing.

I SIT ON the linoleum floor of Sabrina's kitchen; my hands cuffed behind me, my eyes still blindfolded, and my heart still beating with intensity. A cool draft blows toward me from the open refrigerator. *Guys and Dolls* has been replaced by one of Sabrina's many CDs, Marvin Gaye doing his thing, as only Marvin could.

Sabrina is moving around the kitchen making some effort at being quiet, for reasons I'm sure I will find out. What I can hear are the sounds of stuff being set on the floor, of her moving back and forth, and of Marvin singing. Only when I hear silverware clinking together do I start to get the picture.

For anyone who's ever used food as a tool, enhancement or

aphrodisiac for sex, my hat goes off to you. Just make sure to check the dates on your bottles, cans and tubs.

Marvin croons in the background, while Sabrina sits in front of me, she instructing me (in an incredibly sexy tone) to relax and open my mouth. My cuffed hands sweat in anticipation. With a stupid smile on my face, I open up, praying that the first thing she feeds me isn't a Jalapeno Pepper. Cold, soft ice cream is spooned into my mouth, my smile growing wider as Sabrina lets out a nervous giggle.

Sabrina's voice is soft as she gives instruction. "Open wide, Terry. Here's a little something for your taste buds."

A thick pickle slides into my mouth, my tongue first trying to block it, my teeth then baring down, taking a big bite.

"You've been watching *9 and ½ Weeks*," I say, my mouth full.

"I loved Mickey Rourke when I was in college," she admits. "You want a little something to help wash that down?"

I nod a yes, knowing the odds of getting wet are pretty good.

"Here's a little milk," Sabrina whispers as a glass is pressed gently to my lips. "Hope you're not lactose intolerant."

The first few swallows go smoothly, but then Sabrina gets cute and tips the glass higher, allowing milk to run down my chin and neck. She kisses me firmly on the lips, her tongue licking away some of the excess milk.

Merlot, strawberries, whipped cream, a banana with a dash of Cayenne Pepper (Sabrina's sadistic side coming through), yogurt, and a raw egg are what follows, most broken up with kisses, bites and licks. Sabrina slowly pours milk over my head, my protests doing little, and pushes me over onto my side. I hear keys as she straddles me, and the sound of the cuffs clicking free. I instantly pull her down, kissing her neck, my wet hair mopping her floor.

Not five minutes later we're in Sabrina's bed, hands fumbling and mouths locked. Six and a half inches or not, my willy feels like a goddamn hickory stick, the preliminary festivities having turned me on ridiculously. Writhing between Sabrina's legs, with both of us ready to consummate our night's culinary experience, I wonder if Sabrina thinks my dick is big enough. I consider bringing up the subject to her—

And then an unforeseen event starts to unfold: my stomach begins to gurgle, and *not* just a little.

"Is that your stomach?" Sabrina asks in a way that says she's not letting me put that noise on *her*.

"That, or someone else is in here."

Another sound, almost like an animal in pain, echoes around in my belly, my stomach beginning to hurt where my appendix would be if I still had one. Sabrina and I look at each other, our eyes connecting in the candlelit darkness, her expression a combo of concern and shock at the volume of my internal groans.

"You okay?"

I lay down beside her, my stomach quiet for the moment, the pain subsiding. "Jesus! For a second I thought I was having *Rosemary's Baby*. I think all that food's upset 'bout sharing such close quarters—"

My hands and forehead begin to sweat. My stomach starts acting up again—making noises not of this earth—and I am instantly moving through Sabrina's bedroom, naked, half-erect, and in fear of puking all over her nice hardwood floors.

"Baby, are you—"

I slam the bathroom door behind me, reaching the toilet in a nanosecond, only to have nothing come out. Instead, a pressure begins to build in my ass that allows me to empathize with how Mt. Saint Helen's felt prior to her volcanic explosion. I flop onto the toilet, cradling the little trash can in the room in my hands, just in case vomiting comes back into style. Sweat slickens my face as my stomach—

And without further warning—in the home of a woman I'm supposed to be turning on—a level of gas escapes me that will forever belong in the *Guinness Book of Records*. Less like a loud fart, the foghorn that blares from my ass is so fucking noisy I cannot believe what is happening. The sound reverberates around the room like feedback at an old Jesus and Mary Chain concert, all my senses working on overload. I vaguely hear Sabrina's voice in the background; what she's saying incomprehensible. I only pray that death will come quickly. That no one will have to suffer. No one else, that is.

"I'M TELLING YOU, man, I thought I was gonna die. I mean, the smell coulda been bottled and used in terrorist action—"

Isaiah sits on his desktop, waves his hands at me. "I got it. I got it! I'm sure it was as foul and nasty as you say. I don't need all the graphics."

Sitting on his adjustment table, I think about Sabrina and about how I will never be able to face her again in a sexual way. About the mortified look on her face as I exited her bathroom, ordering her not to use it for at least a few hours.

"So it was the yogurt?"

I nod, "Sabrina called the yesterday apologizing. Like she should be saying sorry when it was me who permanently peeled the paint in her bathroom! But yeah, she said that the date on the yogurt was almost three weeks past the safe point. She says she just bought it for that night. That the store must've not pulled it."

Isaiah frowns, "You couldn't tell it was bad when she was feeding it to you?"

"My mouth was a bouillabaisse of foods! *Everything* started to taste funky after awhile."

I glance over at the skeletal systems chart, wondering if I did any permanent damage to myself that night. Or to Sabrina for that matter. I sit there thinking, that if there is a next time, I wanna make the plans. Or at the very least, go over them with her before I'm subjected to anything as scary as the other night. It seems like a reasonable request.

Of course, after tearing up her bathroom like I did, it may not be a realistic one.

Me, my temperamental colon, and my pathetically average penis would most likely have to look elsewhere.

FOUR

Las Vegas, Baby. No!

"THERE'S NO FISH IN YOUR AQUARIUM," Scotty tells me, crouched down and scanning the water.

Isaiah raps him on the shoulder; he and I sharing a look. "Pay attention, genius! Terry's *never* had fish in there."

Scotty stands and looks at me curiously, "Why do you have a fish tank and no fish?"

"It relaxes me before I write. Just looking at the plants, the water," I explain, then add, "Bringing in fish would take it to a whole new level."

"That level being responsibility," Isaiah quips.

We move into the kitchen, where I pass out two bottles of water, keeping a third for myself. Scotty cracks his open and takes a long drink, as Isaiah hops up to sit on the counter, then looks at me.

"So how much you bringing?"

I shrug, "I dunno. Three hundred, maybe four. You?"

"An even grand," Isaiah says. "If I lose it, I'm cool. Long as I keep the ATM card here."

"Must be nice having a real paycheck," I tell him and turn to Scotty. "What about you, tough guy?"

"A hundred or so for gambling. Couple more for some babes if

I feel like blow'n it," he says, wiping his mouth with the back of his hand.

"Hookers, huh?"

Isaiah and Scotty share an odd look, Isaiah turning to me, "Don't tell me you're not up for it?"

I give them a shrug, and wonder if buying sex is something I really want to add to my collection of experiences.

"The jury's still out on that one," I say. "We'll see."

"Either way, in twenty-four hours we'll be in Vegas, baby!" Scotty yells, holding his bottle of water high like a martini in mid-toast. "Yeah!"

Terrific, I'm going to Vegas with a retarded Austin Powers . . .

Isaiah laughs and tips his water in Scotty's direction, my mind on the fact that I can afford a trip to Las Vegas like I can afford a house in the hills. But then I picture the tables, the girls, the lights, the slots, the cheap food, and once again the girls, and remember it's better to regret what you do, than what you don't do.

I walk out of the kitchen and glance at my aquarium, glad that I don't have to worry about who's feeding my fish while I'm gone.

IT IS NEARLY one a.m. After three hours of writing I open a new document and start a letter to my grandmother, feeling the need to fill her in on the latest news in my little life (minus the gaseous incident with Sabrina).

When I was sixteen and things were at their worst with my family, Grandma Kate—herself deeply affected by what was happening—remained an emotional rock. You could go to her and talk, cry, whatever, and she would just listen, giving a level of comfort I have never known from anyone since.

In the past thirteen years I have remained close with her, not letting distance affect us like so many other relationships, where over time you simply talk less and less. I get a note or a call from her at least once a month (her handwriting becoming increasingly tougher to read as she gets older), letting me know how she's doing in her Bridge group, how my aunts and uncles are, and how she'd love for me to come for a visit, taunting me that she can still whip my hide in Gin Rummy.

Having received grandma's latest letter a few days earlier, I decide now is the time to write her, on the eve of me going to Las Vegas. Maybe I can cleanse my soul a little by dropping her a note before I spend the weekend in Sin City. I should have called her before it got so late. Grandma Kate could've given me some lucky numbers to play.

FIVE MINUTES BEFORE Isaiah and Scott pick me up, Drea stops by and gives me five bucks to play on roulette for her, specifically number twenty-two (her lucky number since seeing *Casablanca*). She then tells me to stay out of trouble, her tone strangely maternal.

SOUTHWEST AIRLINES IS nice, cheap and apparently must fill each flight like a goddamn sardine can to maintain that nice, cheap quality. Like cattle we file onto the plane, Scotty mooing loud enough for a few passengers to laugh; the closest flight attendant frowning at him.

"Guess she doesn't like beef." Isaiah says, then advises, "Go all the way to the back, Scott. Bound to be three seats together back there."

The next twenty minutes are spent on L.A.X's "Bermuda Tarmac," an occurrence where no matter how few flights there are taxiing or taking off before you, you and your ass sit perfectly still while what little fresh air there is inside the plane is sucked away and replaced by silent farts and the germ infested exhales of every other passenger.

Scotty, getting fidgety, glances from his window to Isaiah and I. "If we were driving, we'd be half way there."

Isaiah, already impatient, glances at his watch for what has to be the tenth time. "If we were *crawling*, we'd be half way there."

We sit silently for another moment, then Isaiah turns to me, his nose scrunched up. "Did you fart?"

I shake my head no. Next time I fly, I think I'll drive.

LAS VEGAS. DREAMT up by Benjamin "Bugsy" Siegel as an oasis for military types and Hollywood bigwigs to come spend their money, drink and have sex, all under the hot desert sun at a steady temperature of seventy-two air conditioned degrees.

Las Vegas. City of a billion lights, home of the three dollar steak. Where dreams can come true with the pull of a handle or the placing of a bet. All that is needed is a little cash, a little know-how, and lady luck standing over your shoulder. With the right connections you can have it all: cocktails, fine dining, markers worth thousands, and last but not least, hookers. Lots and lots of hookers.

Unfortunately (and typically), Isaiah, Scott and I had no connections. For anything.

We spend the first part of our day walking through the various casinos, each looking more like Disneyland than the other. For every gaming room, there is a show which features either live, exotic animals, or live, exotic dancers. For every high roller we pass around the tables, we maneuver around a roving kid so young, he or she cannot see over the blackjack tables. Somewhere, Bugsy Siegel is spinning in his grave.

Isaiah pulls out his wallet and counts a half dozen c-notes, his eyes then following two little kids as they run between the roulette tables.

I watch the kids as they play and scream as if in *The Mickey Mouse Club*, "I keep expecting to have Goofy or Donald-fucking-Duck pop out and hand me some cotton candy."

Scotty sips the beer he holds, mentions, "That's over at Treasure Island."

"Yo, let's get outta here," Isaiah says over the sound of coins falling into the thinnest of tin. "We need a plan. It's too easy to wander around like these old people. We're here to gamble, meet ladies and enjoy drinks on the house."

"We've already wasted some time, at least an hour or two, I think." I don't wear a watch and locating a clock in a casino is like finding the winning ticket in the New York State Lottery.

Scotty, who is wearing a watch, holds up two fingers, signaling two hours have passed by, none of us any richer or closer to getting laid—either professionally or with a good old fashion horny amateur.

Isaiah heads away from the tables, "Let's try our luck at The Mirage. I've won big on their blackjack tables before."

Both Scotty and I nod in agreement, Scotty bumping into a little girl with a squirt gun on our way out.

THE FOLLOWING SCENARIOS are marked by time to authenticate their existence in what can only be described as "The Three Stooges Hit Las Vegas" (only Las Vegas hit back much harder).

4 P.M. ISAIAH, SCOTTY and I sit at a five dollar Blackjack table, sandwiched between a guy who could be Snoop Doggy Dogg's twin and a woman old enough to have voted for FDR. After thirty minutes of cards, both Scotty and I are down close to fifty bucks each, Isaiah easily up more than a hundred. As he plays, Isaiah constantly holds five chips in his right hand, either out of luck or nerves. The old woman on my right is also up, which isn't a surprise since she's asking for help on every goddamned hand. The way she keeps asking the dealer what to do, this blue-haired fossil makes a presidential press conference seem apathetic.

Our dealer, a sad-faced Asian man in his fifties whips out the cards. My eyes try to keep up with what Sir Speedy deals us. I show an eight and a nine, which is good because you don't need to hit, and horrible because with my luck, the dealer will get an eighteen or better without missing a beat. Ol' Blue Hair asks the dealer if she should hit; she's showing a nineteen. He looks at her with the perfect mix of irritation and pity. Isaiah gets another blackjack, his fourth or fifth, his bet of twenty dollars more than doubling before all our eyes.

"Damn, nigga. You gett'n all the cards!" this Snoop looking guy says. My heart rate instantly accelerates at hearing the word nigger. Subtly, I try and make eye contact with Scott, but Isaiah catches my gaze first, his expression calm, void of any stress.

"Yeah, well, I'm just having a good run, that's all," he replies, turning to face Snoop with a smile.

A few more hands pass, Scotty landing a blackjack twice in a row, while my own pile of chips is nearly depleted. With this round, I show an eleven and decide to double down. The fossil on my right has a three and a four and asks me if she should hit or stay, the dealer no longer willing to answer her questions.

"You're young," I tell her after a sip of my watery gin and tonic. "Live a little, take a card."

Isaiah shows two eight's, with the dealer showing a five. "I'm gonna live a little too and split these beauties," he tells the dealer, and nudges my shoulder.

Snoop sits up, looking from the dealer's five to Isaiah's hand. "He's gonna hav'ta hit," he informs Isaiah. "Let 'em bust and give me and whitey a chance at some a the good cards." The term whitey flies right over Scotty J's head.

Sir Speedy deals Isaiah his cards, the first a queen, the second an ace. Isaiah claps his hands together, a broad smile across his mug.

"You are the *man!*" I tell him, Scotty also bumping him in support.

Snoop, who had a total of nine and is dealt a six, shakes his head in disgust and looks at Isaiah as he whines, "That's bullshit, man. You tak'n my card nigga, when you shoulda stayed on sixteen, let this fool bust!"

I want to say something to this edgy clown, but find myself unsure, not wanting to get into something that makes Isaiah uncomfortable, or worse—

"Excuse me," Isaiah starts, his eyes locked on Snoop's. "Mind if I ask you what your name is?"

Snoop makes a face, sitting up straighter, "What's my name?"

"What is your name?" Isaiah's tone is firm but amiable.

Snoop looks Isaiah over, then answers, "Swank."

"*Swank?*"

"That's what I said. Swank! You deaf?" His tone is thick with attitude, his eyes fixed on Isaiah's.

My sweaty hand picks up my glass, prepared to use it if the situation calls for a fairly scared white guy to step in and get his ass kicked.

From where I sit, I can see the corner of Isaiah's mouth curl up as he smiles. "Well, Swank, we're all sitting here, playing blackjack.

No one's look'n to make any more of it than that. But if you call me nigger once more, I'm going to break your jaw."

"Oh, I get it. You ashamed a where you come from, that it? 'Shamed a who you are?" Swank closes his eyes partway, as if to say he's getting bored with where this is going.

Isaiah leans forward in front of Scotty, getting closer to Swank. "No, that's not it. In fact, it's exactly the opposite. Which is why you're one word from a trip to Las Vegas Memorial. It's your decision, *brother*."

For a moment there is total silence around me. I hear voices and slot machines in the distance, but their volume is strangely low. I see the dealer turn and gesture at the pit boss, a heavy man in a gray jacket. Snoop, a.k.a. Swank, stares at Isaiah, Isaiah's eyes never wavering. Scotty leans further back as if their intensity were forcing him out (that, or he's scared too).

Another moment passes before Swank's eyes brighten, a smile of his own emerging. "Damn, man, iss' cool. I just giv'n you some, that's all. Iss' cool."

The pit boss arrives, his eyes going over each of us like a grade-school principal deciding if he needs to bring out the paddle.

"Everything all right, here?" he asks the dealer.

Ol' Blue Hair raises a wrinkled hand, says, "It most certainly *isn't*. These boys are speaking some gang-related stuff."

Both Isaiah and Swank look at her, bewildered.

I turn to face her, pissed. "After all the help I gave you, you're gonna say that shit? Shut the hell up and learn how to play Blackjack, for Christ's sake!"

Everyone at the table, the pit boss included, stares at me in disbelief. Even Swank's eyes are wide with surprise, at this angry white boy berating someone's grandma.

"What?" I say. "She's driving me nuts. 'Do I hit on ten? Should I stay on two?' Jesus! It's like playing cards with a geriatric Chatty Kathy Doll!"

And with that, I am thrown out of The Mirage, Isaiah now pissed at me for breaking up his winning streak.

5:45 P.M. TO GET the $5.99 dinner special at Mandalay Bay as advertised, not only do you have to get there between four and five, apparently congress has to be in session, there must be a full moon *and* you've got to have Wayne-fucking-Newton's influence, because when our bill comes at the end of our painfully bland meal, it totals more than forty bucks. Isaiah, ever the diplomat, calls after our waitress and asks her about the $5.99 special, to which she, while chomping some gum, explains that we got in five to ten minutes after the buffet special ended. She then throws us a weak smile, and suggests that one of us should buy a watch while we're in town. As she walks off, Scotty holds up his wrist, thinking that if she sees his watch, she'll cut us a break. No such compromise is reached.

"That's seriously wrong," Scotty gripes, and then slides the check toward Isaiah. "Since you won all that green at The Mirage, you get this one, 'kay?"

Isaiah looks at Scotty as though our friend has just admitted to having sex with small animals.

Again, where the bill is concerned, no such compromise is reached.

6:30 P.M. GREED ASIDE, there is also a certain undeniable level of narcissism involved in gambling. From the showoff throwing for a seven at the craps table to the old woman casually playing the nickel slots, we all crave the sounds of others cheering us on, or the ringing of machines that proclaim us what we hope to be—in Las Vegas and in life-winners. Our egos can swell for a few minutes while we're congratulated, our backs patted in support, all the while knowing the elation will only last until either the next person wins more than you, or your winning streak comes to a screeching halt, putting you back in the middle, somewhere between the winners and the losers.

I sit at a progressive video poker machine, feeding quarters like a man possessed. Ten minutes earlier I pulled up four twos, a minor jackpot of seventy-five bucks spewing forth loudly into the thin tin, my heartbeat speeding up as a few bystanders came over to check out the scene.

I've easily put a fourth of my loot back into the slot when an attractive girl in her early twenties sits down at the machine on my right. As if the gods of Vegas were smiling down on me, not only do I now have this sexy fresh-faced brunette beside me, I hit four aces, setting the bell ringing again, with another decent payoff dropping out. The brunette glances over, smiles at me, me shrugging as if to say I'm more lucky than good.

You are more lucky than good.

Several minutes pass; my fresh-faced neighbor and I have each hit a few small jackpots, twenty bucks here, thirty bucks there, each of us nodding and smiling at the other in approval.

After examining her latest hand on the screen, she looks at me and asks, "What do ya think I should do here? Keep the jack and queen or the pair of twos?" Her tone is sweet and has the slightest southern twang to it, which makes her that much more attractive.

I turn to her and catch a glimpse of her eyes, a soft blue-gray. "You wanna play the odds. Keep the face cards. 'Jacks or better,' you know."

This southern beauty taps her forehead, "Oh, duh! I 'spose I could've figured that out on my own. Sorry."

"Don't worry about it," I say, looking at her for longer than I should. "Truth is, what I know about this game wouldn't fill the first page in a how-to book."

She smiles at me, "You seem to be doing pretty good there."

I try and think of some snappy retort, my well of sarcasm momentarily empty, then realize I need to introduce myself. After all, this girl here seems to be enjoying my company, having a bit of fun. Never being especially courageous when it comes to taking chances with an attractive stranger, I cannot count how many times I've regretted not risking the first move, never knowing—and always wondering—what might have come of it, simply accepting, instead, that nothing happened. Unlike Isaiah and Scotty, hookers are not a serious option as far as companionship, I hoping instead that a situation like this would present itself, maybe me finding the balls to just—

"My name's Terry," I say, deciding not to overanalyze it further, and just offer my hand.

"I'm Melanie," she says, shaking my hand and smiling a little. Her eyes glance down shyly. "Nice to meet you."

"Nice to meet you too, Melanie."

Yes!

That's one small step toward manhood, and one giant leap toward shattering the great fear barrier. This simple moment has now become a blueprint for future similar scenarios. The crazy part is how easy that was. That this girl and I could now spend the better part of the day together or simply part ways after a few more minutes wasn't nearly as important as the fact that I'd stepped up to the plate and taken my turn at bat. The pathetic part is that it's taken me twenty-nine years to get to the point where most sixteen-year-old guys already are. Never mind, I've arrived, and now I'm going to get to know this Melanie, my gut telling me she's as interested as I am, she being the one, after all, to sit down beside me—

"Yo, Mel! Keep those three fours," an undeniably male voice calls out behind us. "If you git another one, we win somethin' like fifty big ones!"

Before I can fully turn around, two thick arms reach around my poker playmate's shoulders, a guy the size of a Volvo leaning down to kiss the top of her head. And like that, I am cut off at the knees. One small step for manhood has become more like one small stumble.

"Hey baby," Melanie says to her Hulk, then turns to me. "This's Terry. He's helping me with my poker."

I give him a nod, trying to feel as macho as possible, the guy's eyes going from me to my video screen. "Dude, those're some bad cards. Git some new ones and start over," he advises.

He doesn't know the half of it.

8:20 P.M. HARD ROCK Hotel/Casino. If I had a buck for every chained wallet, goatee—sporting cat in this place I wouldn't need to keep gambling. The Hard Rock is cool because most of the people who hang out here weren't alive when either Kennedy was assassinated, the average person being in their late twenties (as opposed to the MGM Grand where the average person was old enough to remember when there *wasn't* a Las Vegas), and fairly attractive. The downside is the casino isn't all that cool. The place comes off more like one of those Euro-trash restaurants on the

Sunset Plaza, except that the music is slightly better and, of course, you can gamble.

Over the Hard Rock's sound system, Paul Westerberg sings about his "first glimmer of light." We have been here fifteen minutes and Isaiah—growing increasingly impatient with the possibilities before him—has already mentioned driving out to Pahrump twice. When asked about his fascination with paying for sex, Isaiah gives Scotty a stern look, explaining that no matter what, we all pay for it, directly or not, depending on the girl, and how much she makes you jump through hoops before doling out her love like a poker dealer does cards.

"Besides," he adds. "I've always been curious 'bout those chicken ranches out there. I wanna see what's up."

I look at him, "What's up is they're not selling chicken."

"Well, I'm ready for it, whenever you guys are." Scotty announces, his eyes lighting up a bit too much. "I think it'll be cool."

"Let's hang out a little while, kids," I offer. "There are some girls here worth getting to know. And I wouldn't mind gambling some more."

Isaiah smiles at an attractive black girl, her eyes on his. Saying nothing to us, he walks off, keeping pace with the girl, whispering something to her that gets a laugh. Amused at his instant change of heart, I watch as they disappear into the crowd.

I look at Scotty, "Roulette?"

"Roulette," he agrees. "Can't do any worse than I did at Blackjack."

I suddenly remember the fiver Drea had given me, and decide this place is as good as any to try for her. All five dollars on one number, twenty-two, and all at once.

"Remember *Casablanca*?" I ask.

He glances at me, his gaze then moving on to two curvy blondes playing a Sid Vicious slot machine. "The movie?"

"No, the PTA group. Yes, the fucking movie!"

Scott, distracted, turns to me and gestures toward the two girls. "They're giving us a friendly look. Dude, we should head over there."

Apparently, number twenty-two on the wheel will have to wait.

11 P.M. TIME DOES not exist inside the casinos of the world.

Clocks never hang in view of the players. God forbid some guy realizes he's late getting home to tuck in his kid, after all, his wallet still has a few twenties in it. As long as you have money, and a limited amount of will, time loses its hold on you.

Long after Scotty and I moved on from the girls (both were annoyingly drunk and one snorted when she laughed, like Chrissy from *Three's Company*) at the Sid Vicious slot, we find ourselves with sore backs and even less money, courtesy of Wanda, the Cyborg Dealer. Wanda, who has less personality than a canned ham, systematically beats Scotty and I over an hour of blackjack. She almost never busts or wins with anything less than a nineteen. When I explain to her that she could earn more tips by occasionally showing mercy, she just looks at me with the same vacant expression she wears while dealing out our losing cards. I count my chips and realize that not only is the small pile of winnings I so recently won completely gone, but I've also dipped into another c-note; my wallet feeling very thin in my pocket.

The latest hand she's dealt me is a queen and a nine, a hand that most would feel good about. Scotty sports an eighteen, and judging by the tense expression on his face, he is prepared to hand over his money right now. A four then joins Wanda's face card, my breath held as I pray she busts with her next card. Instead she pulls a seven, her faceplate remaining emotionless as she takes our dough.

Scotty mutters a few four-letter words under his breath as I collect what's left of my money and slide a dollar chip over to this dealing machine.

"Here's a little something Wanda," I tell her, coolly. "Put it toward having a personality program installed."

Walking away, we spot our long lost friend Isaiah, his own face longer than ours.

"Nice to see you're still alive," I say. "You realize we've been in this shithole for a hockey season?"

Isaiah frowns and takes a swig off Scotty's beer. "Don't nag me. I wasted two-plus hours working that girl, and she tells me she's got to go to bed!"

Scotty J's eyes light up, "Cool. Sounds like you're in."

"Does it look like I'm *in*? I'm stand'n here talk'n to you, aren't I?"

Clearly someone's having a bad night with the ladies. I pry further anyway. "She's staying here, in the hotel?"

Isaiah nods and continues to rant. "Says she's running some half marathon at seven in the morning. What fucking half marathon? This is Las Vegas. In *June!* Even at seven a.m. it's three hundred mother-fucking degrees outside. She shoulda told me up front, saved me a couple a hours a work." He glances around, his eyes wide with frustration. "Let's blow this place; it's time to get serious."

Scotty and I look at each other, both knowing what "serious" means. We are about to embark on a journey where far too many men have gone before. We are heading for the land of plenty, as in plenty of hookers.

I glance at Scotty's watch and consider mentioning that it's getting late for a road trip, but something tells me Isaiah is going anyway. Scotty also appears pumped for the upcoming events. I convince myself that this could work into my column someday and decide not to be a killjoy. Besides, the further I'm from the tables, the less likely Wanda or any other evil dealers are to tap into my near depleted funds.

Of course, last time I heard, sex with a professional wasn't exactly free, either.

12:30 A.M. HIGHWAY 50 through Nevada is considered the loneliest stretch of road in America. Half past midnight, I wonder if the 160 West toward Pahrump isn't a strong contender for taking over that claim.

Isaiah drives his rental car like a man on a mission (which he is, actually). We pass a lone sign reading "Pahrump 32 miles." Were it not for the incredibly potent hooch we picked up just outside of Vegas, I'm sure the sign would have added to my nerves. Taking the bottle from Scotty, I force down another swallow, which burns my throat and makes me wonder if this is the kind of alcohol that laid waste to so many American-Indians.

"Half hour and we'll be in the arms of some fine loving women," Isaiah tells us, the earlier edge in his voice now gone.

Scotty takes the fire-water back and sips it gingerly, his eyes wide and eager as he proclaims, "I'm thinking about getting a three-way. You ever had a three-way, Terry?"

I write a sex column for a Los Angeles based magazine. When I'm not working the self-deprecating humor, I will occasionally throw in bits of actual experience, hoping it will add some authenticity. As yet, I have never written about participating in a Menage a Trois.

"The closest I've come is playing Australian Doubles in tennis," I admit, feeling like an "L" for loser should be stapled to my forehead. I grab the bottle of hooch and down a sizable slug, my throat and nasal passages permanently cleaned out.

"Well, don't worry 'bout it," Isaiah offers. "Whatever you decide, you knuckleheads are gonna love it. Key is not to get all nervous and shit."

Easy for him to say. Isaiah's been with more prostitutes than Jimmy Swaggart.

1:35 A.M. WE PASS a sign stating San Francisco 340 miles. We are either lost or we've traveled through a black hole. Frustrated with our current situation, Isaiah stops the car on this incredibly empty stretch of Highway 160. Only a handful of stars provide light, the air around us black.

"How did we miss the turn off?" Isaiah asks aloud.

I glance around, the darkness and silence (with the help of the firewater hooch) closing in on me, "I don't know. But we should at least keep the car moving. Sitting here like this makes us perfect targets for guys with chainsaws and freaky eating habits."

Scotty, his own tone a bit edgy, mumbles something about the Blair Witch.

Isaiah pulls a U-turn.

2 A.M. WE PULL into the gravel driveway of "Bessy's Chicken Ranch." My hands are slick with sweat, my heart is racing with anxiety. Only three cars, including ours, are parked in the lot, one is on cinder blocks.

"You sure this's it?" Scotty J asks. "Seems kinda deserted."

Isaiah turns off the motor, points knowingly at the sign. "See where it says Chicken Ranch? They're not selling McNuggets."

I take a final slug of the hooch, finishing it off, and realize I'm feeling ridiculously nervous, even scared. I have no idea how this is supposed to go; a dozen questions are bouncing around my skull. Do I pay the girl before or after our little rendezvous? Should I tip, and if so, is fifteen percent acceptable? And what about the fact that she *is* a professional? Am I going to come off like some awkward schoolboy? Is she going to be rating my performance? Or will she lay under me, bored, occasionally stealing a glance at her clock like Jane Fonda in *Klute*, hoping I'll finish so she can catch the end of TNT's late night horror marathon?

We stand outside the car, Isaiah, Scotty and I all giving each other a knowing look. Scotty's eyes seem to gleam in anticipation, while my own are buggy with apprehension.

"Play it cool my pale brothers," Isaiah starts. "I hear these places make it real easy. So keep it nice and simple."

Scotty glances around, a goofy smile on his face. "Cool," he says as we move for the doorway, where my heart speeds up even more. "I hope they'll let me get a three-way."

We move for the entrance, my anxiety increasing ten-fold.

I hope I don't vomit on their floor.

2:15 A.M. IS WHAT the ornate clock on the mantel reads. Sitting like schoolboys, side by side on an orange sofa from the mid-seventies, Isaiah, Scotty and I listen to a woman who resembles Bailey from *WKRP* explain to us how the way-too-near events will transpire. Holding a small bell in her hand, our tour guide speaks softly as I glance around the room. It looks like something from a twenty year old *Sunset Magazine*. The air is thick with the smell of Patchouli oil.

"Now when I ring this little bell, several ladies will come out and stand before you," she explains in a tone that makes me feel mildly retarded. "And then you gentlemen will be free to choose whomever you would like to meet."

The word "meet" hangs awkwardly in the air as she continues.

"Take your time. When you have decided, simply point, and you and your lady will be on your way."

Scotty's hand juts upward like Sam Donaldson at an old Clinton press conference. "Can I pick two women? You know, for a three-way?" His tone is as excited as an eight year old after ice cream. I secretly hope that the giant Cherokee security guard at the entrance will barge in and shoot him dead.

Instead, our tour guide gives our goofy friend Potsy Webber a sweet smile, and tells him a menage a trois is perfectly fine.

Ring. Ring. Ting-a-ling.

Oh shit, here we go . . .

My hands are soaked with perspiration as Isaiah and Scotty share an excited look, then all eyes move to the end of the hallway as the sound of whispering floats down to us.

Several girls in their early twenties file out of the hallway, and slowly form a single line before us. My mind tries to compute the absurdity of this sight; it coming off like some kind of R-rated Bataan death march. All the girls are wearing nighties; their bodies covered just enough to keep your imagination from clicking off. All are at least reasonably attractive, but I instantly sense that none of these girls—not one—is coming off as sexy. Without an air of mystery, or uncertainty, the moment is strangely . . . bland. I figure this makes sense since this scene has all the spontaneity of a *WWF Match*. The girls look at us, most appearing tired. One girl unsuccessfully tries to fight off a yawn, while another wipes sleep from the corner of her eye. Again, I look at the clock on the mantle. It's 2:22 a.m.

What in the hell are we doing here?

"I think I'll take you," Isaiah says, his voice cutting into the uncomfortable silence. He sounds like a kid picking a goldfish. An instant later, he and a pretty girl with long red hair slip down the hallway.

And then there were two, just Scotty and I. My eyes fall over each girl, not wanting to wimp out on trying this experience, but not that amped about it either. Just truly nervous.

You mean terrified . . .

Scotty points at the only African-American girl, a smile on his face, "I would like to hang with you," he says, the giddiness in his voice rising as his finger moves to a chesty girl with short brown hair. "And you too, please." At least he's polite.

At this moment I feel incredibly alone. I can only imagine what these poor girls must be going through every time some clown like me shows up here. All eyes on moi, I want to break into a giggle and explain that I'm the token gay friend along for the ride. Getting the feeling these girls are anxious for my pansy-ass to hurry up and choose, I stand and gesture toward this waifish blonde in a loose fitting nightgown.

"Feel like playing naked Twister?" I ask, hoping some humor will break the ice. I get a weak smile and nothing more. At 2:25 in the morning, who can blame her?

2:26 A.M. BLONDIE'S ROOM reminds me of my sister Tricia's (which freaks me out even further). The décor is a combo of teeny-bop girliness and of someone wanting, needing, to come off as an adult. An Ansel Adams print hangs over the north wall, above her queen-sized bed. I hear the door closing; I turn and Blondie and I awkwardly share a nervous smile.

"I feel like a schmuck for coming here so late," I say, then realize my lame choice of words. "Sorry, no pun intended."

Blondie moves to her dresser and picks up a thin folder. "That's okay. I've got tomorrow off." She hands me the folder, its cover pink with large red letters reading MENU. "I'll get to sleep in."

I look at Blondie, my anxiety briefly replaced by confusion until I open the menu up and read with amused bewilderment what is before me. For a moment I think this is part of some practical joke, that what I'm reading over can't be for real. I glance back at Blondie, her face free of any signs that the gag's on me. Looking again over the folder, I scan over my choices, trying desperately not to giggle like some freaked-out schoolboy.

BESSY'S CHICKEN RANCH

. . . SERVICES . . .

Missionary Position $200
Missionary and ONE Additional Position $300
TWO Positions, Client's Choice $375

Anal $375

ONE Position and Anal $450

Specialty .... above prices plus $50

Oral Pleasure $150

Manual Pleasure $100

Menage A Trois (1st hour only) $650

". . . we take requests . . ."

I stare at the prices for what feels like Ronald Reagan's time in office, realizing my c-note now carries all the weight of Monopoly money. Oh so slowly, I lower the menu and give Blondie, who is sitting ever patiently, a smile.

"And all these come with fries and coleslaw?"

An actual laugh escapes this girl; a genuine smile on her face, instantly sucking away all of the tension I feel. Her face lit up—the front momentarily gone—I find myself swooning at this girl's natural beauty, the way she holds her hand to her mouth, as if trying not to come off too human in front of a client.

"I've gotta be honest here," I start, not a hundred percent sure where this is going. "All I've got on me is a hundred dollars, and as attractive as you are, I can jerk myself off and it won't cost me a nickel." I hold open the menu, point at the price list, "I mean, look at these prices, at what you guys make! I'm considering putting on a dress and moving in with you."

Blondie gives me a friendly grin and lays back on her bed, her head propped up on one arm. "Oh, it's not so much. It pays bills, tuition, and lets me go out a couple nights a week."

Tuition? I picture a lecture hall filled with clean—cut boys and girls in their school's colors, sweatshirts and ball caps abound, with Blondie in the middle of everyone, taking notes during some calculus lecture, wearing the same nightgown she currently sports with me.

We look at each other, my anxiety nowhere in sight, completely drained away. In these few seconds, this girl has shown an honest, unguarded sexiness that makes me want to take her out and get to know her. I saw *Pretty Woman*, I know this shit is cheesy. But I feel strongly about it, like Blondie and I are connecting, no different now than two people in a club or at a party. From a neighboring room another girl's stereo plays Nik Kershaw's "Wouldn't It Be Good." Thinking about the chance I took earlier today with the girl at video poker, I decide I'm meant to keep giving it a shot, to step out from the shadow of doubt. The perfect chance. The perfect old song playing as background music.

I take a deep breath, look warmly at her, and my babble begins to spew forth. "Seeing how I'm a broke moron and you're already awake, what do you say to us going out to the local Denny's, or whatever it is you guys have out here in *Deliverance* country, and we get a bite to eat? I'm not a registered pervert, I swear. I just feel like a jackass for wasting your time and think you're a very decent person. I know I sound cheesy. Extra cheesy, probably, but . . . what do you think? Some pie and coffee on me? It could be fun. At the very least, interesting."

I pull out my wallet, hold out the c-note, and begin to dance slowly with it, a stupid grin plastered on my face.

Blondie is laughing as she stands, moving toward me. She takes my arm to get me to stop dancing and then leans forward, kissing my cheek.

See, McGuire, you can be charming on occasion.

Our eyes meet and I think I'm falling in serious lust, a feeling that just as quickly dissolves once I realize she's shaking her head no and motioning for me to open her bedroom door.

2:45 A.M. THE ENTRANCE room has a small bar, a pool table, and a large TV that currently shows more snow than picture. Rejected, dejected, and feeling pissed off about Richard Gere being a better pick-up artist than I am, I sip on a bottle of bad beer, all the while under the eagle-eye of the Bessy's stone-faced security guard. Bored, I want to offer to play billiards with him, except I'm nervous that he'll take it wrong and beat me to death with a pool stick.

The greeting room door opens and Isaiah comes out. I look at the wall clock behind the bar, perplexed. Isaiah's face is as somber as a condemned man's.

"Lemme guess. You didn't have enough money, either?"

Isaiah takes my beer and has a huge drink of it, his tone depressed as he explains, "I had plenty, man. Problem is, I got, well . . . the girl checks out your dick before she agrees to have sex with you. To check for STD's and shit."

"And you've got something?"

"No, I don't *got something*!" Seriously defensive, Isaiah goes on with his story. "I got a birthmark."

"A birthmark?"

"A birthmark! I'm black. My dick is black. Except for about a half inch on the side of it, where it's lacking color. Looks like a white dude's right there. Kinda."

I look at my friend, still unsure. "And she had a problem with a two-toned schlong?"

Isaiah shakes his head, eyes the security guard just long enough for me to get nervous. "She just wanted to be sure that was it. So she got that woman who gave us the instructions, you know, with the bell? So now there's two women going over my johnson like a science project, neither wanting to believe what I was telling 'em." Isaiah frowns, has another sip of beer before adding, "I got the boot."

Without a clue as to what to say, I stare at the snow covered TV screen, wondering if Isaiah and I could be any more pitiful.

Probably not.

3:40 A.M. SCOTTY J finally returns, tucking his American Express card into his shirt pocket. He looks ten pounds lighter, and on his face he sports the mother of all shit-eating grins.

I consider asking the Indian security guard to shoot me and end my misery right now, and then decide I should just head back to L.A., and continue my pathetic life. Besides, he'd probably only wing me in the neck or something, leaving me wheelchair bound for the next forty years. What I need is one good bullet straight through the heart.

Of course, I don't have that kind of luck. Las Vegas has hammered that point home quite effectively in the last twelve hours.

FIVE

When Terry Met Chloe

IMPORTANT AS FAMILY IS, THERE ARE TIMES when visiting with them, either in person or by phone, feels torturous. The conversation I'm currently suffering through with my pop is one of these times.

"Did you check out Legacy?" Pop asks, as if I should have a clue as to what he's talking about.

"What's a legacy?"

"Legacy. The *golf course*. You can see it as you're flying into Las Vegas," he explains. "Good course. Has a couple of great Par Three's."

I contemplate telling him that the closest I got to any hole was a student-prostitute in Pahrump, then decide against it in a hurry. "Dad, you know how I pretty much only hit the links with you and Uncle Dave?"

"Yes?"

"Well, neither you nor Uncle Dave were with me last weekend."

For a moment, pop is silent, probably stewing over the fact his son is both a non-golfer *and* a smart-ass.

"I don't know how you could afford Las Vegas in the first place, the money you make," he says, his tone telling me he's sulking on the other end of this fiber-optic line. "You need a more stable career if you're going to travel so much."

I am now irritated, not only because the nagging has already begun, but also because once again the old man with the nine handicap has struck a chord.

Just as I come up with a good sarcastic reply, the call waiting "beep" sounds off, saving my pop and me from that much more tension.

"Dad, I got another call coming in, you wanna hang on?"

"Sure."

I click over and say hello.

"When you guys walk in, there'll be a tall guy with a clipboard. Your names are on it," Drea tells me. "Be sure you're on time."

"Do we need I.D.?"

"It's a play, not a sex club," my laconic friend says.

This, I decide, means no I.D. is required.

"We'll be on time. You better not stink," I warn. "I'm bringing rotten eggs and old fruit."

"Thanks for your support."

"No problem. I gotta go, my pop's on the other line."

I click over and decide to play nice with pop, and end our conversation civilly.

"That was Drea," I say, trying to shift him away from his last thought.

"How's she doing?"

"Good. I'm going to see her in a play tonight."

"You kids," Pop starts in, his tone condescending. "You all want to be writers, actors, musicians. Whatever happened to becoming doctors, lawyers? Real work."

Apparently, civility is no longer on the menu.

GETTING READY FOR Drea's play, I stand in my bedroom, dabbing a little cologne here and there. I put on a fresh shirt and look at my *Raiders of the Lost Ark* poster, at Indiana's confident eyes, his sure smile. I stare at the poster for a long time, lost in thoughts about choices I've made, and about people I used to know and have fallen out of contact with. For a moment I think about my sister and what she might be up to right now. My thoughts shift to my mom, more specifically, to how fast the time has passed.

Feeling a *Felicity* moment coming over me, I move to my closet and dig out my old senior-high yearbook. Plopping onto my made-for-one bed, I slowly flip through the pages, immediately enjoying the reunion.

I find my old track team photo, nearly forty of us dressed in our goofy green practice sweats. I glance at the student-council page, my cheesy grin embarrassing now, but full of pride and conviction then. While flipping toward the journalism page I happen across a few more intimate faces from the past. Memories of friends and crushes come rushing back as if the eleven years since graduation had been instantly wiped away.

I stare at the senior photo of an old girlfriend, Melinda Rhodes, my mind clicking on our first date, how I took her to see Bryan Ferry in concert, the two of us smiling like goofballs at each other the entire night.

Gazing at Melinda's picture, I wonder if she went to our ten year reunion. I blew the reunion off last summer, in part because the idea of going back to high school seemed about as much fun as being re-circumcised. But in truth, I was also anxious about going back as a barely successful writer and sometime video store clerk. I didn't want to bullshit people about my life, nor have to explain why my career is moving at the rate of slug with a hernia.

Still, it might've been cool to see some of the old crowd. They might've understood . . .

Twenty minutes pass before I realize the time. I jump up and finish getting ready, not wanting to be late and suffer Drea's wrath.

Where does the time go?

THE PLAY DREA is in sucks. Isaiah and I endure this pretentious piece of shit like a pair of real troopers, both wanting to bolt for the door, but staying to support our actress friend instead. The only actors who don't stink are Drea (praise Allah) and this little brunette with a great chest and these gorgeous almond shaped eyes. When the tortuous proceedings finally end, the entire audience seems to breathe a collective sigh of relief, each person forcing themselves to give an enthusiastic round of applause. Isaiah and I whistle at Drea; her eye catches us as we do this, and the tiniest of smiles spreads across her face as she takes her bow.

Afterwards, in the theatre's parking lot, as other actors and audience members schmooze, Isaiah and I stand off to the side. We wait patiently for Drea to come out so we can congratulate her for shining far above nearly everyone else.

"Were you nodding off in there?" Isaiah asks me, a yawn escaping him. "I thought I saw you fading."

I shake my head, "I was slipping into a coma from being so goddamned bored. Fucking thing ran like *My Dinner With Andre* on slow speed."

Isaiah points at Drea as she and the brunette from the play head over.

"Hey! Thanks for hanging out after," Drea says, her face warm and bright from performing. "What'd you guys think?"

Isaiah and I exchange a look, his expression telling me to answer first, that he'll base his statement on how well I articulate mine.

Come on, Mr. Mouth, think of something nice to say . . . NOW!

"It was—what's the right—it was interesting," I start, feeling lame for not being quicker with something positive (or at least convincing). "Definitely interesting."

"It wasn't that good tonight," Drea concedes. "There're still some kinks the director hasn't worked out."

"Really," I say, throwing Isaiah a quick glance. "You . . . you couldn't tell at all."

"But you know what," Isaiah pipes in, blowing by me in the compliment race. "Both of *you* were great. The best! Easily, the best of everyone."

Drea and the brunette, who is even better looking up close, thank him.

"Terry, Isaiah, this is Chloe," Drea says, getting the introductions underway.

"How you doing?" Isaiah asks, shaking her hand.

"Good, thanks," she says. Her voice is soft but strong as she glances from Isaiah to me. "Thanks for coming tonight."

I offer my hand and Chloe's gently receives it as we make eye contact. "Isaiah's right. You two really were the best out there. By far."

Way to sound like Isaiah's puppet, jackass.

For one shining moment, I become lost in Chloe's beauty, the warmth of her dark eyes, the milky white glow of her face. And her lips, the way they turn up just a hair at the corners of her mouth.

Drea slaps my shoulder, yanking my eyes from Chloe's face, "Since we impressed you both so much, you boys can buy us a couple of drinks. What do you say?"

"I say you've got a deal," Isaiah tells them.

"Long as we can get your autographs," I add, my line coming off more lame then funny—which happens more often than I'd like to admit.

"Deal," Chloe replies playfully while Drea rolls her eyes at me.

"We'll be back," Drea tells us. "We have to finish packing up our costumes. Give us ten minutes."

Both Isaiah and I nod in understanding. The girls head back inside the theatre. Chloe gives us one more smile before disappearing backstage.

"That girl is death!" I proclaim, leaning on Isaiah for support.

"She's a cutie."

"A *cutie*? The Olson Twins are cuties. *Stuart Little* is a cutie. This girl is death!"

Isaiah smiles and nods. "I had a feeling you'd like her, soon as we saw her on stage."

"Your feelings were correct, sir!"

"Just calm down a little," he advises. "You look like a kid in a candy store. All giddy and shit."

Feeling giddy, I start singing Bow Wow Wow's "I Want Candy."

Isaiah takes a few steps away, not wanting to be associated with the freakish white boy singing bad Eighties music in the name of newly discovered lust.

TWO HOURS AND a dozen drinks later, the four of us decide it's time to call it a night. I don't want to.

Chloe is the one for me. For now, anyway.

At this point in my life, as I edge toward my fourth decade on this planet, there have been very few girls I've known that made me feel nervous, excited, terrified, lustful and special all at the same time. Four girls, in fact, until now. After one hundred and twenty minutes of drinking Guinness and sharing stories, I know in my gut that this girl is someone truly amazing. I could stare into her dark eyes for another two hours without missing a beat. I could listen to her talk, to the way her voice cracks as she's about to laugh. Truth is, I could listen to Chloe *belch* for two hours without missing a beat.

Both Isaiah and Drea are onto me. Drea is lightly kicking my leg beneath our corner booth at Tom Bergen's, her gesture a signal that Chloe is interested too. Isaiah keeps mentioning my column as if to say, this guy's going somewhere (even at only six-fifty a month), that I'm not the typical L.A. flake. Secretly, I love my friends for their efforts, appreciating their attitudes and support.

Now on the sidewalk, with the traffic on Fairfax still heavy for the hour, we all begin our good-byes. Drea and I hug warmly; she whispers that I should get Chloe's phone number, that she has a pen in her car if I need it. Isaiah and Chloe give each other a hug, Isaiah telling her again what a nice performance she gave in the play earlier.

"I'm going to start the car, Chloe," Drea tells her. "Terry, call me tomorrow." Drea walks toward her car, Isaiah accompanying her, giving me a big Cheshire Cat grin.

"I'm gonna wait by your car, man," he says. "Protect Drea from anyone shifty."

Chloe and I stand a foot apart, my head buzzing from all the Guinness, my hands slick from nerves.

"I'm really glad we got to see you and Drea perform tonight," I say. "You were both terrific. Really, I mean it."

Embarrassed by my compliment, she squeezes my arm and glances at the ground. In this moment I want to press her against the bar's outer wall and kiss her as though life depends on it. Of course, I don't, my "Id" instantly ashamed of me.

"You're sweet, Terry," she tells me, her deep dark eyes on mine. "I had a really nice time with you and Isaiah tonight. Drea too." She laughs, then adds, "Do you maybe want to go for coffee or something sometime?"

Something? Sometime?

If you don't seize this moment, you should be lobotomized and neutered.

The following words pour from my mouth; "Absolutely, I would. And not something sometime. Let's see each other in the next few nights."

Jesus, McGuire. You just acted like a man who knows what he wants.

The earth stops spinning for one single moment as Chloe leans forward and kisses me on the corner of my mouth. I am suddenly sixteen, feeling like a goofy kid with a big cheesy crush. I want to bottle up this feeling and keep it on display for the times ahead when life is darker, more depressing. I cannot help but marvel at how one tiny action can carry so much weight.

"I'd like that too," she says, a sly grin on her face as she turns for Drea's car.

It takes me several seconds before I do anything; walk, think, whatever, which is when I realize that I didn't get her number, nor did she get mine. For a moment I panic, but then I decide that this is going to happen. This thing, growing out of nowhere only a couple hours earlier. I actually calm down, knowing Chloe and I will see each other again. And in the next few days too.

Standing on the curb, in the warm summer air, I feel proud for behaving like the man I someday could be. Indiana Jones would approve. At the very least, he wouldn't bash me on the head and shove me into a spinning propeller.

MY CLOCK READS three-thirty in the morning, the red numbers the only light in my room. I lay awake, my mind on the night's events. I had planned on simply going with one friend to see another perform in a local play. Instead, I have become seriously infatuated with a girl who before eight p.m., I didn't know existed.

Closing my eyes, I can picture her face, the curve of her body beneath her hipster clothes. I wonder why I didn't get her number? I go over the kiss she gave me again and again, my brain doing instant replay like *Monday Night Football* showing Joe Theismann's leg breaking.

Part of me wants to call Drea, see if Chloe said anything to her, but then I remember I'm twenty-nine, not twelve. That kind of behavior at my age—and at this hour—is closer to stalking than sweet.

The clock reads quarter to four when my eyes close for the final time, Chloe's kiss the last thing I think of before drifting off to sleep.

THE DREAM COMES to me like a haunted vision. I'm having sex with an ex-girlfriend, a girl I broke up with in the name of needing to be single. Slowly her face morphs into another ex, Melinda Rhodes, whom I drove away with endless erratic behavior. As Melinda's face morphs into Janet's, I suddenly notice my mother from the corner of my eye, sitting on this mauve loveseat, making me a peanut butter sandwich. As I pump away on Janet, who is now morphing into another ex named Rochelle, my mom asks me if I want some Fritos with my sandwich, then tells me not to blow it with Chloe, like I have with all the other "nice girls." I turn back to face Rochelle and see that Chloe is now beneath me, eyeing me suspiciously, her mouth full of corn chips. Mom then tells me not get any crumbs in the bed.

WHEN I WAS eighteen and on my first date with Melinda Rhodes, I knew she was something great and that she too, felt pretty good about me. As the date came to an end, I walked her to the front door and just when you might think a goodnight kiss was coming, I offered my hand like a proper English Gentleman, told Melinda what a great time I'd had, and said "goodnight."

While what I'd done was a crap shot, the move did make Melinda want to see me again even more, her curiosity sparked as to what the deal was. She knew I liked her. She knew I'd had a great time that night. And she knew I wasn't gay—I assume. Needless to say, when I did kiss her at the end of the second date, Melinda greeted my lips with voracious intensity. Ever since that night, if I like a girl (I mean really, really like her), then I'll play this little game, the results so far being a consistent big winner.

After my first night hanging solo with Chloe, Drea calls at midnight to ask me what's with the handshake thing. Apparently, Chloe had called her and wasn't sure if I'd had fun. Explaining my tactics—and sharing the Melinda Rhodes story—Drea pronounces me as wildly fucked-up, then swears to say nothing about it. She then warns me that if I didn't at least kiss Chloe on the next date, she'd have me flown out to Fire Island where I could really relax, and get to know some of the boys.

After we hang up I realize Drea is right; the games and tactics should end. Melinda Rhodes was a long time ago. I'm supposed to have progressed by now.

Don't dick around with petty games. Be a man. Go for it!

I'm almost thirty. I should have a grip on my feelings. I've had a dozen chest hairs since the first George Bush was President.

Be the man, McGuire. Go for it!

Christ, I feel like a jackass . . .

AT THE END of life, all we have are our memories; many good, many not so. A first trip to Disneyland. Your first time riding a bike without training wheels. Family trips to the ocean. Your parent's losing battle with cancer. Making the dean's list. Getting a driver's license. Your first sexual experience. Your first time to Pahrump.

All these things are remembered not so much in their entirety, but as specific moments or days, these smaller memories as strong as the experiences themselves. My Grandmother once said, "if at the end of your time, you can recall more nice days than bad ones, you've done all right."

This second night out with Chloe, I know that the way I feel as we talk over our third round of red wine, is something I'll always look back on with a smile.

Originally, the plan was to meet around seven and grab a quick bite before hitting a movie. Three hours and one employee shift change later we still sit on the patio of the Sonora Café on La Brea, neither of us giving a damn that the movie part is out.

Listening to Chloe talk about her family, her parents divorce, her fledging acting career and her love for orchids and Tom Waits,

I cannot think of anywhere else I'd rather be. The more she tells me, the more I want to hear. The way she laughs at my lame jokes and comments, the upward curl at the corners of her mouth, somebody should stick a fork in me, because I am done! This vision has me hooked.

When I yammer on about my life; my mom, my pop's golf and shit like that, her eyes light up as she listens. I tell her about my writing and she orders me to give her back issues of the magazine, admitting she read the last couple articles only after a friend of hers mentioned them. Her praise makes me feel a little awkward, but also like a fucking king. I know I'm sitting with the finest catch in the room, and she actually *is* interested in me, in my little life. I want to reach across the table and kiss her, more and more regretting my hand-shake move from the other night.

"So, I wanted to ask you, Terry," Chloe starts, her speech careful, a slight smile on her face. "The other night? When we were saying good-bye, you shook my hand. Do you remember?"

Is this girl psychic too?

I take a nice long sip of wine and then a deep breath, a smile of my own creeping across my face as I nod, "Yes, yes I do, Chloe. I was just thinking about that right now."

Chloe's large eyes squint a bit as she grins, "Oh, really?"

"Uh, huh. I was thinking that clearly I *wasn't* thinking," I tell her. "I wanted to kiss you, but thought I'd wait, maybe see if you'd notice."

Chloe sips her wine, her eyes on mine, my heart speeding up. "I did."

"Then maybe I made the right choice."

"I wouldn't say that," she says. "But it did make me wonder."

Sitting here with a few glasses of Merlot in my liver and an oh so slight buzz in my brain, I debate moving this conversation into the serious flirting zone or easing down and keeping it mild.

Fuck it, we're going serious.

"And what exactly were you wondering?" I ask, then add, "Please make your answer as R-rated as possible."

Chloe smiles, taking her time with another sip of wine. "I'll tell you what. How about I don't give you an answer quite yet, so you can feel a little of what I did the other night, when I was hoping you'd kiss me instead of that boring handshake."

Chloe reaches across the table and sips my wine, her gorgeous eyes gleaming mischievously over the side of the glass.

I look at her, conflicted. I don't like her answer all that much, but I love the way she delivered it.

A TWENTY MINUTE drive, complete with a pit-stop at Sal's Liquors on Colorado, and Chloe and I are walking down Santa Monica beach with an open bottle of Merlot, drinking directly from the bottle like a couple of winos. A half moon and a few stars give us light as we move down the beach, the sand cool on our bare feet. Knowing how polluted this beach can get, I silently pray I don't step on something nasty, killing the night's mood and winding up at St. John's Hospital.

We talk about everything, from serious subjects like her dad's drinking and my mom's illness, to ridiculous things like which *Godfather* movie is better, part one or two. Our current rant is on the ever-increasing need for the good people of L.A. to surgically enhance their bodies, my own brash opinions paling next to Chloe's razor sharp outlook.

"We're always saying how 'it's what matters on the inside' or 'happiness comes from within,' B. S. like that," she says as I take a swig of wine. "But the truth is, as a society we're concerned with appearance more now than ever. Which makes me believe that as a whole, more people are more miserable now. Like what's going on in their heads is so depressing, they can only improve the shell of their lives. The hypocrisy makes me wanna—"

I pass Chloe the bottle, nudging her, "I think you need a drink."

Chloe stops in her tracks, takes a long swig. "Sorry, I tend to get on a soapbox when I've had too much to drink."

"That's okay, I tend to get drunk when I've drunk too much."

Chloe smiles, brushing her hand against my face. She then plops down on the sand. I slowly sit beside her, my eyes going from her face to the blackness of the water, the sound of the waves relaxing as I concentrate on them for a moment. In the silence, I realize I'm comfortable with this, our silent agreement to just sit together, letting time take us where it will. Like Uma Thurman says in *Pulp Fiction* (and I'm paraphrasing, of course), "There's nothing like hanging out with someone who knows when to shut the hell up."

After a few minutes and a few more swallows of Merlot, Chloe's head comes to rest on my shoulder. "McGuire," she starts, "You don't mind if I call you McGuire, do you Terry?"

"Nope."

"Good. I like it. McGuire," she whispers. "It's a nice name."

I turn my head a little and lean in close to take in the scent of her hair; "Chloe's not too bad, either."

"No, it's not. I hated it as a little girl, but it's grown on me. Better than Stacey or Lucy."

We sit quietly for the moment, listening to the surf. In the distance, somewhere behind us, a girl is laughing, calling out to someone named Steve.

Chloe moves her head and looks at me as I sip from the bottle. "Are you planning on kissing me sometime soon?" she asks, her voice soft.

I turn to face her, her eyes deep pools of black under the night's sky. I want to come up with something quick and witty, but am unable to find the words. Saying nothing, I put a hand to her face and guide our mouths together, figuring this should count as a yes.

In my humble opinion, the way to tell if someone is good in bed is fairly simple: they have to be a good kisser. Kissing is such an overlooked art, the masses concentrating way too much only on the actual act of sex. But truth be told, if someone sucks at kissing, odds are they're pretty bad at everything that follows. A good smoocher knows when to apply the tongue, how much saliva should be shared, and when to pull back, allowing for both air and an increased desire for more kissing. A good kiss is special, an act that both parties must enjoy. These are fairly basic rules that seem to mystify far too many people.

Sitting under the stars, our mouths together and our lips working passionately but gently, I have absolutely no doubt that Chloe's great in bed.

NO MATTER HOW emotional, intimate or private a night between a guy and the girl he likes is, that guy is going to blabber and boast about it to at least one of his friends, turning that special moment into something more like a play by play from *Deep Throat* or *Seymour's Swinging Sluts.*

Sitting on the edge of Isaiah's desk, I describe my night with Chloe in all its glory, Isaiah's interest evident by the goofy smile he sports while listening.

"They're like these, these perfect sized breasts that are actually real! You know, just the slightest hint of a droop, and how then they arc upward?"

"Oh, yeah," Isaiah and his goofy smile say.

"She has such a great body, I felt like I should bolt for the gym before we went any further," I tell him, my mind filled with Chloe's image, her shape and her scent. "And her ass! Her ass is like . . . like this nice round scoop of Vanilla Ice Cream!"

"Oh yeah!"

"I just kept looking at it, like maybe I was imagining things. Like it wasn't 'sposed to be so . . . *amazing.*"

Isaiah stands up from his adjustment table, rubs at the back of his neck a bit, "So, you're definitely gonna see her again?"

"Definitely."

"And you think this could go somewhere, you and she?"

A goofy smile of my own appears at the thought, my brain going over Chloe's face, and the way her messed up hair made her even sexier for our second round of sex. "Oh yeah."

Isaiah grabs two Cokes, tossing one to me. "So she's an actress who has a Psych degree and a tremendous body, and *doesn't* leave a dozen hickeys all over your skinny frame?"

"Exactly," I say, and pop open my soda.

"This mean you done with Sabrina?" A good question my Chiropractic caring friend poses.

"Uh, I hadn't thought of that one," I confess, mulling it over for a few seconds. "There's no rule says I can't see them both, make a decision if Chloe and I get more serious. Remember, so far Chloe and I aren't much more than a great one-night stand. A ridiculously amazing one, but a one-night stand all the same."

How's that for rationalizing?

Isaiah gives me a look, "Fifty dollars says you and Chloe are serious within the week."

"The week? You ought to give me more credit than that."

"I hear it in your voice," he says. "Saw it the night we met her. Trust me, Terry. You take this bet, you lose."

I think he's wrong, but considering I'm working at Todd's video store tonight on account of I've got less money than most homeless folks, I decide I need to start betting like I need a bag on my hip.

THREE DIFFERENT CUSTOMERS at Video Schmideo tell me that I'm glowing, two of these cats asking me who the lucky guy is. The way I feel, I consider telling them the lucky guy is me.

It is you, McGuire.

Driving home I stop off at Ralph's and grab a pint of Ben and Jerry's Heath Bar Crunch and a six pack of Guinness, knowing that by morning I'll need to workout for three hours just to atone for my gluttony.

I'm in my apartment less than ten seconds when I scoop up the phone and check my voice-mail, hoping Chloe's on it.

Instead, it's Drea telling me about this new guy she's dating, a casting agent who specializes in getting old Jewish men onto sitcoms. Scotty is next, reminding me we're running tomorrow afternoon; my eyes falling on my brew and ice cream as I erase his message.

That's it, no other calls. No Chloe telling me what a great time she had last night. No Chloe calling just to say hi. No Chloe at all. My elation evaporates to neurotic disappointment as I pop the cap off one of the Guinness.

On the television CNN is broadcasting locally, covering the story about what is now the third poor bastard found murdered and dumped along Mulholland in the past three months. The report keeps cutting back and forth between pictures of the victims, the specific places each was found, and strangely picturesque shots of Mulholland, as if to give the story a "How Could This Happen In Such A Beautiful Place" feel. The reporter stands along Mulholland, his hair being blown by canyon winds as he tells viewers how both the L.A.P.D. and the F.B.I. are now working in association.

I mute the TV and close my eyes for a moment. The writer in me begins to come out as I think about these killings. I'd always wanted to write a screenplay, but never found the right story, not to mention the right amount of motivation. Maybe if I take this story off the TV and give it some serious tweaks, maybe I can try a mystery for my first script. 'Course, what those tweaks are, I haven't got a clue.

Maybe you should concentrate on you next column, seeing as how it's due in a week . . .

I rub at my eyes and shift on the couch, my mind drifting elsewhere.

Back to Chloe.

I want to call her. The clock on top my TV reads eleven forty-five. It's probably too late to call. Besides, I left a brief message earlier. Calling a second time would be a breech of my dating guidelines.

McGuire, you are such a moron.

The phone rings. I move for it like Maurice Greene. Hovering over the receiver like a hawk, I let it ring a second time before picking up, trying to come off as mellow, calm.

A moron and a fake.

"Hey you," Chloe says, her voice shooting my mood back to the elation level. "I hope I'm not calling you too late."

You can call at four-fifty in the a.m. if you want.

"No, it's all right," I say, keeping my voice even and calm. "I'm glad you did."

"Yeah?"

"Yeah."

"I was just calling you back," she tells me. "And I wanted to say how much I liked last night. Like being an understatement."

I feel like a fucking champion hearing her admit this.

"I had a great time too," I say. "I don't wanna come off as cheesy, but I thought about it a lot today."

"Yeah?"

"Yeah."

There is the slightest pause before she speaks up, "You think maybe you want to spend tonight together, too?"

Does the Pope wear a funny hat?!

"I'd like that. Give me twenty minutes to head on over."

"I'll come to your place, if that's okay with you?" Chloe says.

Does the Pope wear a funny hat?!

An hour later we lay on my couch, sharing the Heath Bar Crunch, our legs entwined, our faces inches apart. I feed Chloe a bite of ice cream. She kisses me warmly, her mouth and tongue cool from the Heath Crunch. Pressed against her, I wish we could hang like this for a week straight, eating, fucking, watching bad TV, talking, fucking. Another bite of ice cream and Chloe takes the spoon from me. One of her thin, arched eyebrows arches a bit more.

"You wanna have some real fun with this stuff?" she asks.

Knowing this girl is something incredible—and that the expiration date on the ice cream is good and safe—yes, I am very ready to have fun.

ANOTHER HOUR HAS passed. Chloe and I lay close on my little bed, our skin stuck together from a combo of bodily fluids and ice cream. A few candles burning, we stare at one another in the flickering light.

"If I tell you something McGuire, you promise not to wig out?" Chloe asks, her voice quiet, extra soft.

"Long as it has nothing to do with roadkill or Jay Leno naked."

She bites my chest lightly, then says, "I know this sounds weird, given that we've just met, but . . . I really want to keep seeing you. I *really* want to."

No matter how much I'm into a girl, when certain "committal type" words—or mindsets, for that matter—creep into the picture, my instinct is to either fuck it up, or bolt for the door, thereby fucking it up anyway. So naturally, when Chloe says this to me, my stomach tightens a little and I can't help but avoid looking her in the eye just yet, my brain working hard and fast on the best possible response.

Don't freak on her, McGuire. You like this girl a lot.

I sense Chloe's eyes on mine as I stare at my Kobe Bryant poster, trying to find his signature in the candlelight. I can feel the seconds passing, my mind failing me big time.

"McGuire?" Chloe breaks the silence, a hint of anxiety in her tone as she speaks. "Please don't feel like you have to say something back. I only want to be honest with you. To share what I'm feeling."

Honesty. Sharing.

Serious girl words.

I shift on my little bed, my eyes finally focusing on Chloe's. For the moment we simply stare at each other. I want to speak up and say something profound, but in this moment, with all our concentration on one another—and with the perfect lighting—I decide to just stay the hell quiet, and let the look between us speak volumes.

And you call yourself a writer?

Chloe's lips rise oh so slightly in the corners of her mouth as we keep our moment going. She looks so great lying here, next to me, her eyes deep dark pools of emotional beauty.

Suddenly, my mind flashes on what Isaiah said, about Chloe and I getting serious. In this moment, as I finally move in for another kiss-breaking the hypnotic spell between us—I silently thank whoever's listening for keeping me from taking Isaiah's bet.

Fifty bucks is fifty bucks!

A
U
G
U
S
T

SIX

Love Is a Four Letter Word

"REALLY? 'I LOVE YOU'?" ISAIAH ASKS ME, a big dopey grin on his face as he sits on the ground, stretching before our run. The reservoir is fairly free of people, given the warm morning—most of the regular runners apparently waiting for an early evening jog, when the sun has finished its shift for the day.

I stand with my legs spread shoulder length apart, and do some stretching of my own as I explain to him what happened: Yesterday, Chloe had stopped by unannounced, which normally would have been okay, except for the fact that yesterday was the anniversary of my mom's death. I had spent the day keeping to myself, not so much out of mourning as I just didn't feel like being around people. I had already spoken with my sister Tricia, my pop, and my Grandma Kate, and I was having a tough time shaking off my melancholy frame of mind. So I figured I'd watch *Terms Of Endearment*, do some writing, and get to sleep early. Keep it simple and get a good fresh start on tomorrow.

Then the doorbell had rung.

Thirty seconds after Chloe came in, she knew something was bothering me. So I gave her the Cliff-Notes version of how my mom had died when I was sixteen, barely a week after I got my driver's license. How the big C (that's Cancer to the rest of you) had been diagnosed in both her breasts only a year earlier, and that despite a radical double mastectomy, mom's battle came to an end in early August, thirteen years ago today.

Isaiah gives me this look; his eyes narrow as he speaks, "You know better than to tell a woman about a dying parent, or any kinda stuff like that. *Of course*, she's gonna say she loves you!"

"I didn't tell Chloe to get her all lovey-dovey," I say in my defense. "I just thought she had a right to know. Besides, I wasn't going to lie to her." I start running in place for a few seconds. "How was I supposed to know she'd throw out the L-word?"

"Think about it, Terry," Isaiah starts. "Women are naturally more emotional than guys. Not in a bad way, but they are. And when you start acting all sensitive—and you're a *man*—well you might as well hang 'em up right there, cause love is bound to come around knocking."

I stop running in place and mull over his words.

"And you two were in bed when she told you?"

I nod yes, picturing the scene between Chloe and me.

Somewhere overhead, a blue-jay cries out, as if mocking me for my predicament.

"It was a nice moment," I admit to my friend. "You know how it is, we're having this ridiculously romantic sex where we're both taking it slow, and—"

"And bam!" Isaiah says, slamming a fist into his open hand for effect. "She loves you!"

I look at him and shrug. "Yeah, yeah, yeah. I know what you're going to say, cause I've already thought it twenty times. It's awfully soon to start throwing around the I love yous."

Isaiah cracks his neck, the loud popping creeping me out. "How long since we met her at the play?"

"Almost a month." I tell him, not liking the fact that the L-word has reared it's uncomfortable head before the thirty day mark.

Isaiah gives me this odd grin, says, "Long as you don't say it back until you're ready, you'll be all right. A little awkward, but all right."

I don't say anything, apparently for too long because he looks at me with worry in his eyes. "You *didn't* say you love her, right?"

"No, no!" I fire off. "But it did seem to make things . . . *weird* . . . for a few seconds. Me not saying it back."

"Of course, it did."

I stand, thinking about Chloe, the sun warming my face. "This's my fault. I shouldn't have brought up my mom dying, that's all."

"Like you said, you were being honest," Isaiah points out. "No shame in that."

"Yeah, I 'spose you're right. Damn. Why couldn't Chloe just tell me she's sorry? Why the 'I love you'?"

Now Isaiah begins to run in place. "Friends say they're sorry about stuff like that. Girlfriends and lovers say they love you."

Great. Maybe you should write that down and keep it for future reference . . .

I look at my friend and nod. "I just think that now we've crossed some kind of new line, you know? Like things can now only go in the direction of getting more . . . *complicated*. It's kind of frustrating. We were getting along so well, why'd she have to bring love into it?"

Isaiah looks at me, then points toward the sky. "Anyway, it's getting hotter out here. You wanna run this thing before we melt?"

I nod and the two of us are off, my brain going over Chloe's words again and again.

Isaiah glances over at me and says between breaths that he's sorry about my mom dying of cancer, that that's fucked up.

I look at him, curious. "I've told you this stuff before."

"Yeah, you have," he says, agreeing. "I'm still sorry about it. I don't like hearing 'bout people suffering and shit."

"Thanks. It was a long time ago," I tell him. For a few seconds we both run in silence, the moment seeming too heavy for exercise. Naturally, I decide to lighten things up a bit. "Just don't say that you love me."

A couple more strides and Isaiah punches me in the arm, mentions something about me nearly owing him fifty dollars.

Somewhere above us another blue-jay cries out.

ONCE INSIDE MY apartment, Drea walks straight into the bathroom. In her hands are a black picture frame and matching soap dish. I follow her into the bathroom—secretly thankful I hadn't just stunk it up—and watch as she moves to the toilet, glancing at the *Sports Illustrated* on the back of it.

"Glad to see you're keeping the *Playboys* out of sight." Drea says, her tone a funky mixture of appreciation and parental concern. She then takes the picture frame and places it strategically on the bathroom counter—to the left of the sink, a few inches from where the counter meets the wall.

"Drea? What're we doing?" I ask, already nervous about the answer.

Drea picks up the nub of soap that until now has always rested freely on the counter. She puts it in the shiny new black soap dish and sets it to the right of the sink. This apparently creates a *balance* within the room. She then surveys the new additions and smiles with approval.

"One small step at a time, sweetie," Drea says, and pats my cheek before heading back into the living room. "Make sure you put an appropriate picture in that frame. No sports crap."

I mumble a thank you and offer her a beer or bottled water.

"Actually, I'm okay. I've got about two minutes before I gotta get going. I'm hitting an audition for this national Pepsi commercial. It's over the hill, so I want extra time in case of traffic."

"Good luck," I tell her. "Hope you kick some soda-drinking ass!"

"Me too," she agrees, then plops on my couch. "So I met a guy the other night."

I sit next to her, my curiosity sparked. "Really? Who's this lucky cat?"

Drea's face lights up as she starts in, her hand running through her platinum hair, out of what I can only assume is a combo of nerves and excitement. "His name's Patrick. He's thirty-two and works at Red."

"He's a waiter?"

"He manages the bar," she clarifies. "Which is an immediate plus."

I smile at the thought. "Free drinks."

"Exactly. You should see him. He's so beautiful! He has these great cheekbones and really nice arms. And he's so sweet and funny."

"And he's not an actor?" I ask.

"Sweetie, this is L.A. Of course, he's an actor," Drea explains.

"He was on *Law and Order* last season for an episode. He played a suspect in this double murder. He got to get beat up by the old cop on the show, said it was a lot of fun."

Drea is beaming as she talks, which tells me that she really likes this guy. I decide not to mention Chloe's "love" comment, not wanting to eclipse Drea's current excitement.

"He sounds cool," I say. "How'd you meet him?"

"Lyndsy and I had dinner at Red a couple nights ago, and I kept looking over at him." Drea explains in a way that makes me think there's more. There isn't.

"And that's it? You hit it off just like that?"

Drea grins, her sweet eyes wide with pride. "Guess he thought I was cute."

Women—especially attractive, charismatic ones—have no idea how easy they have it when it comes to meeting men. There are always guys out there, ready and willing, to meet some new babe, and no guy worth his salt would *ever* walk away from the opportunity. And because of this fact, nearly any woman can always meet a man. True, he may end up being a jerk, or hung like a hamster, but at least women have the ability, and the luxury, of finding out. Guys, on the other end, have to scratch and claw their way into half the dates they land, women being a bit more hesitant when it comes to taking a chance. Then again, the way so many of us man—boys behave, who could blame them?

I did an article on the subject for my column in *Angelino Style* several months back and actually got a few pieces of near—hate mail, the consensus being I had no concept of what hell women go through when dating. 'Course, being a guy, I didn't take the criticism too seriously. I was just happy I had physical proof that a few people actually *did* read the column.

"So when are you two seeing each other again?" I ask Drea, who quickly stands.

"Tonight," she says, palming her car keys. "We're going for sushi in Westwood. I was hoping maybe you and Chloe would want to come along. You two are still ga-ga for each other, right?"

Ga-ga?!

I pause, thinking for a moment. This might be a good thing, being out with Chloe in a very public setting, allowing us to have fun, but also keeping us in an arena where the "I love yous" might be kept to a minimum. Plus, I can meet this Patrick and make sure he isn't some douche bag just trying to get into Drea's pants.

"Sounds fun," I say, fighting the need to invalidate the ga-ga comment.

"Great." Drea says. "I'll call you with the details after my audition."

"Break a leg," I tell her. "Figuratively, I mean."

With Drea out the door I think about the evening's possibilities, then head for the bathroom to look over my new picture frame and soap dish. Staring at the frame, I realize I'm at a complete loss for what kind of photo belongs in the bathroom anyway.

Maybe Isaiah would know.

SUNSET SUSHI EAST is one of those current hot spots where everyone goes for the first six months, until the next "current" hot spot opens up.

Drea's new beau, Patrick, used his restaurant connections to get us a table without having to wait at all, which made the twenty or so people waiting in the entrance less than happy.

So, amidst plates of freshwater eel and a spicy yellow fin tuna, Drea, Patrick, Chloe and I continued our pseudo-heated debate about the current state of film and Hollywood in general, the conversation fairly animated thanks to a few rounds of Saki chased with Asahis and Sapporos.

"The way the Industry pumps out so many movies these days, it makes sense that there's more trash, simply due to the law of averages." Patrick remarks, his eyes going over each of us as he speaks.

So far, Patrick seems to be a decent cat, whose greatest flaw is that he doesn't appear to have any. He's a good looking guy and is very attentive to Drea, which allows me to like him more than I had expected—the fact that he's attentive, not good looking.

"I'm not so sure," Chloe starts in response to Patrick's comment. "There is definitely an across the board dumbing down taking place in movies. You even see it by watching the previews. Previews used to be half the fun of going to the movies. Now they give away the entire story in two minutes, as if they don't trust us to figure out what looks good on our own."

"It all comes down to one thing," Drea says after a shot of Saki. "Money. The Industry is a business, and as long as they get people's money, they're going to keep doing it the same way."

"I agree with that," I chime in and give my friend a look, before adding, "But you'll never get people to boycott going to the movies. So, what you have to do is not worry about it, and if need be, work outside the current system, and hope that the product you create will develop a following."

"And that's where independent film and film festivals become so important," adds Chloe, who by the way, looks fucking great in her silk shirt and leather pants.

I bite into my eel roll and chase it down with some Saki. Looking at Chloe, at her face, her eyes, and the way her long dark hair is loosely piled a top her head, I want to blow on out of here, maybe take her back to the beach, or someplace equally moody. For the moment, I'm pretty sure that Chloe's happy with the way things are going, that the other day's love comment was perhaps no more than a fluke based on my mom's death.

Get over it, Terry. She said "I love you." And only one time. It's not like Chloe admitted to sleeping with sheep . . .

"Terry, how do you like writing for *Angelino Style*?" Patrick asks me, pulling my mind back to planet Earth.

As I turn to look at him, I catch the ring finger of his right hand digging in his nose. And it's not just a quick scratch either, but a three or four second probing that makes me wonder if anyone else at the table sees this. Both Drea and Chloe seem perfectly content, Drea even biting into her yellow fin roll, which—knowing Drea—would not be happening if she had just spied her date mining his nose like a man searching for gold.

"Well," I start, still thrown by the visual, "It's good. I'm not exactly earning a living at it, but getting paid to do something you love is a pretty terrific feeling."

"I hear you, man." Patrick says, his finger momentarily back in plain sight.

"What's your next column going to be about?" Drea asks me,

a glint in her eyes, since she knows I don't talk about the column to people until it's done for that month.

I smile at my trouble-making friend and ask, "Are you looking for an ass-whipping?"

Drea gives me a little smile. "Just putting you on the spot, sweetie."

"How come you don't tell people what you're writing?" Chloe asks.

"Because if people already know, they'll be less inclined to pick up the magazine," Patrick says.

"You're a good guy, Patrick," I tell him, then turn to the girls. "Not to mention, I lose interest if I blow my creative wad by yapping about it too much."

Chloe rubs a foot against my leg, giving me a sly grin. "We wouldn't want you to do that."

I flash her a cheesy smile and glance back at Drea and Patrick—
What the fuck?

Again, Drea's date is using his ring finger to clear out whatever nuclear waste he's got hidden up his schnoz. I watch in horror as he continues his voracious quest, and then decide to try and abort his effort.

"You all right there, Patrick?" I ask, bringing the attention to him.

Not missing a beat, Patrick's finger slips from his nose and, along with the rest of his hand, reaches for the eel plate and picks up another roll, where he proceeds to take a large dramatic bite. If I wasn't fairly sober, I'd swear I was either hallucinating or this guy was trying to fuck with me.

"Terrific," he answers, and then licks his fingers.

And still, neither Chloe nor Drea catch any of this.

Please, dear God, don't let Drea kiss this guy in front of me . . .

I look at Chloe, who is working on her last bite of eel, her face showing no sign of having seen anything funky. Paranoia creeps into my brain as I wonder if this is some kind of extreme prank being played on me by everyone else in the restaurant.

"You guys want to order anything else?" Patrick asks thoughtfully, oblivious to his own nasty-ass behavior (I assume).

"God no, I'm stuffed," Drea says.

"I think I've reached my limit," Chloe agrees. "Thank you."

"Terry?" Drea asks. "Are you still hun—"

"Nose!" I say quickly, panicky. "I mean, NO, I'm full. Fine! Really. Thanks."

Did you just say nose instead of no? McGuire, you are a complete moron . . .

I give Patrick a quick look, waiting for the next nasal adventure, deciding that if he goes for it, I'm going to take my bottle of Asahi and smash it over his head.

Desperate times call for desperate measures. Even in the latest dining hot spot.

AN HOUR LATER, Chloe and I sit on the campus of U.C.L.A., in the middle of their soccer field. Spread out on a blanket that was in my Cherokee, Chloe and I lounge in the darkness, sharing a bottle of Chardonnay. Chloe laughs at me as I complete my rant about Patrick's nasal fixation.

"I can't believe I didn't notice this." Chloe says, in between laughs. "You're sure he wasn't scr—"

"Chloe, the guy was knuckle deep! I kept thinking his finger was gonna get lodged in there. That we'd have to call the fire department or something," I tell her, then take a heavy sip of my wine.

Chloe watches me for a second, glances at her own paper cup of vino. "You know, Saki, beer and white wine can't be safe combination. Not if you're trying to avoid a hangover."

I take another sip from my cup, and pick up the bottle. "No, it can't. You want a refill?"

"Please," Chloe nods.

I fill her cup and the two of us toast to a beautifully cool night, good sushi, and the fact that neither of us picks our noses that much.

"After this round you wanna head to my place?" I ask, my hormones starting to lose their patience.

Chloe gives me this mischievous little grin, and sets both our drinks to the side of the blanket. She then moves her foot to my crotch, slowly applying pressure against my little side kick.

"Why do we need to go to your place?" she asks me while unbuttoning her silk shirt.

I glance around the darkened field, no one in my line of vision. "Long as an impromptu rugby scrub doesn't break out, I 'spose right here is fine."

Chloe now straddles me as I lay back on my elbows. Her shirt opened, she takes one of my hands and runs it across her chest.

"It's better than fine," she says, her dark eyes on mine. "It's perfect."

And then, not ten minutes later, while Chloe and I make the most of U.C.L.A.'s practice field, Chloe tells me—for the second time in two nights—that she loves me.

AT SCOTTY J's pad, Pete plays Missile Command while Scotty and I set up for a much-needed night of poker.

Normally a weekly event, our foursome hadn't convened for cards in close to a month, most of my evenings taken up with writing, the video store, or most likely, Chloe. Finally, at Scotty's and Pete's urging—and Isaiah's threatening—I figured it was time for some old fashioned male bonding.

One thing I've always detested about certain guy friends is their ability to fall off the face of the Earth when they're into some new girl. Not only does it show weakness, it says a lot about their apathy toward keeping up friendships. In the past month, I was beginning to turn into one of these morons, enough of one to warrant serious doses of self evaluation.

Not to mention poker with the boys.

"Where the hell's that black man?" Scotty asks while plopping a fresh, unopened pack of cards onto the table.

Working the arcade game's roller, Pete says something about the traffic being extra thick tonight, that there was a fender bender on Laurel Canyon when he was coming over the hill.

"Some jerkoff probably nailed a coyote," Scotty says, and heads into the kitchen.

Pete's game ends, and he also moves to the kitchen, where he grabs a couple of Guinness and hands one to me. "I hear you and this woman you're seeing are pretty serious?"

I sip my beer and sit down at the card table. "Yeah, I guess we're moving into *Exclusiveville*. Something like that, anyway." Even with friends, I'm less than thrilled about admitting to a "serious" relationship.

"Don't believe him, Pete," Scotty pipes up, pulling out one of his patented nasty-ass cigars. "Terry's already hooked. And there ain't no way he's wiggling off the line."

"You've got to smoke that thing, don't you?" I ask Scotty, gesturing to his stogie, and then turn back to Pete, shrugging. "I dunno. Chloe's great. I mean, I really do like her. A lot more than anyone else in a long time. But there's still this little part of me that isn't fully ready to make the commitment."

"That little part is called your *dick*," Scotty explains in his typically tactful way.

Pete nods, smiles. "You're looking to keep your options open."

"Yeah, maybe. Probably. I don't know." Realizing both Pete and Scotty are right, I find myself uneasy, not wanting to admit that all my freaking about Chloe's "I love you's" may be nothing more than me wanting to keep my options open. Then again, maybe I'm simply not ready to go to the next level, not wanting to force anything that doesn't come naturally, on its own.

Fuck, this shit is confusing . . .

I take a long swig off my Guinness and move for Missile Command.

"THINK ABOUT IT, they're very few words that carry as much weight," Isaiah says, then tosses another buck onto the ever-growing pile of cash. "You say 'I love you' to someone and they're not ready to hear it, you're risking the entire relationship. They might bolt on your ass." Isaiah sips his beer before continuing. "Imagine it. Here you are. You've just made this big Ol' declaration of love, and the mutha's running for the door!" he laughs a little. "That's fucking tragic."

Isaiah's words immediately begin to eat at me. I try to concentrate on my hand.

"I once dated this girl, Treena Tartaglio, who said she loved me after two dates. You believe that? *Two dates*!" Pete says, his tone a combo of fear and amazement.

"Treena Tartaglio!" Scotty J. says, then adds, "With a fucked up name like that, poor chick was bound to be whacked in the head."

"This coming from a guy whose last name is *Janwankowski*," Isaiah says, then looks at Pete. "So what happened? How'd you handle it?"

Pete shrugs, "I said how nice that was, told her I'd call her, and never saw her again."

"Glad to hear you dealt with it like a man," Isaiah mumbles, sarcastically.

"Tartaglio?" I ask Pete, he nodding a yes. "Yeah, I remember her name in the paper. Threw herself off the top of Mann's Chinese Theatre. Something about a broken heart . . ."

Scotty and Pete laugh as Isaiah continues the "love" discussion, apparently wanting to hammer a few points home. "Seriously, when a woman says it, we're dicks if we don't say it back right away. Like we're uncaring assholes."

"We *are* uncaring assholes," Scotty points out.

"And don't forget we hate commitment," I add.

"Exactly!" Pete says, also tossing another buck onto the mound of cash. "As if there's no middle ground. You either commit or there's no trust on her part."

"You know what the monster difference is?" I begin, pausing long enough to sip my Guinness and get the boys' attention. "Between guys and girls? Guys want a girl who'll be loyal, like a partner in crime, or a best friend. But we want that loyalty *before* we make a commitment. And girls want you to commit *before* they give you their loyalty. They want you to earn it from them."

For a nanosecond, the room is quiet.

"That's not bad, Terry," Isaiah says.

"You should have your own relationship column," Scotty jabs.

I glance at him, "Never happen."

For a few seconds, we all concentrate on our cards, as if any of us really knows what the hell we're doing.

"Still," Scotty starts in, breaking the silence. "We could all be chicken shits for whatever our own personal reasons are. Nobody wants to get hurt, you know? A few years ago, I dated this girl for six months, and towards the end of it we were both saying we loved each other."

Isaiah looks at Scotty, trying to read him. "If you were both saying 'I love you,' what the hell'd you break up for?"

In this moment, I expect Scotty to say something like her tits weren't big enough, or that she dumped him because he was "loving" a couple other girls at the same time. Instead . . .

"She moved back to Wisconsin. Her little brother had been in some shitty car wreck and got fucked up. In a wheel-chair and everything. She moved back to help her parents take care of him for a while," Scotty pauses for a second, setting his cigar in the ashtray. I can almost feel his thoughts as he stares downward, before adding, "I was pissed that she left, but how can you argue the reason. Fuck. It took a long time to get past it."

"She never moved back? To L.A.?" I ask.

"Nah. She ended up falling in love with some trainer for the Brewers. Last time we talked, she was getting engaged to him," Scotty says, then quietly adds, "Lucky bastard."

And there it is. The seemingly least sensitive guy in Los Angeles county just leveled the emotional playing field. I feel like giving Scotty a hug, but don't want him to think I'm belittling what he's told us.

Isaiah stands and gives us all a look, apparently unsure how to react—for once. "Who wants a beer?"

Pete raises his hand.

"Me too," I say.

Isaiah looks at Scotty, "Scott? You want one of those urine flavored beers you love?"

Scotty shakes his head no, looks at his cards. As Isaiah passes by him, he gives Scotty's shoulder a squeeze, as if to tell him he's right: that we've all been down that emotionally brutal road too, that he's not alone.

When Isaiah and brew arrive back at the table, Scotty picks up his cigar and begins puffing away. "Let's get this game going. I need you fucking clowns to finance my rent this month."

Pete, Isaiah and I give each other knowing looks. Isaiah

mumbles something about kicking all our skinny white asses with the hand he's got.

Okay, sentimental moment over.

THE NEXT DAY, while going over notes for my column, the phone rings and I make the rare choice to pick it up, hoping it's Chloe.

"Hey," Drea starts in, "I'm gonna ask you a couple questions, and I want simple, honest answers, okay?"

The edginess in her voice tells me that a sarcastic reply wouldn't be appreciated at this moment. So I tell her "no problem," and prepare for her inquisition.

"You go down on your girlfriends, right? You give them head?" Drea asks.

Whoa! Whoa! Where is this coming from?

"Um, Drea? Are you recording this—"

"Keep it zipped, Terry," she cuts in. "Remember, simple and honest."

"Yeah . . . yes. Unless there are some specific reasons to not do so, I have been known, on more than several dozen occasions, to give the girls I sleep with head."

Assuming there is a heaven, please let Mom not be looking down and listening right now. Please let her be playing Ping-Pong with Janis Joplin or someone . . .

"And you *like* to give head, right? You're not doing it out of obligation or anything else?" Drea sounds like a psychotic Bob Woodward the way she poses her questions.

"I pay taxes out of obligation. I make car payments out of obligation," I tell her. "I don't give head out of obligation."

For a couple seconds, Drea is silent on the other end. Paranoia slowly takes hold of me until she speaks again.

"Okay, I gotta get going. Thanks sweetie."

She hangs up, leaving me to wonder what in the hell that was about. I look at my fishless aquarium, at the plants and gravel, trying to remember exactly how I came to have the circle of friends that I do.

The telephone rings again, breaking my concentration.

"Hello," I answer, figuring it's Drea. It is.

"You know how much I love you, and value our friendship, right?" she asks me, her words making me smile like a goofy kid.

"Most of the time, yes."

"And how much I appreciate your honesty?"

I glance back into my aquarium as I answer, "Yes."

"Good. Just making sure," Drea says, then adds, "I gotta go."

I don't want to nag her, but I have to ask, "Are you okay?"

"I'm fine. I'm a little cranky with Patrick, but I'll figure it out. Call you later."

We hang up and I stand there, realizing that if someone's got my phone bugged, they may never have a need for those nine-hundred sex lines again.

AFTER A COUPLE burritos at Poquito Mas and seeing Sleater-Kinney at the Roxy, Chloe and I sit at Red Rocks on Sunset, our evening going perfectly. We drink Mellonballs, our inhibitions slipping further away with each tasty sip. Chloe's face is glowing with happiness. Over the stereo system an old INXS tune plays. Watching Chloe, I cannot help but feel proud, proud that I'm here with her, barely noticing any other girl in the place.

Chloe orders another round of drinks from our waiter, insisting that she pay for them. "McGuire, you're a struggling writer who's moonlighting in a video store," she says, a little too easily for my own security. "It's totally fine with me to share in paying for stuff." Chloe then leans in closely, playfully batting her eyelashes for effect as she adds, "Long as you keep giving me orgasms on a nightly basis."

Knowing she's joking (hoping anyway), I kiss her and say she's got a deal. But my brain replays the words "moonlighting in a video store" again, the need for the word LOSER tattooed across my forehead suddenly growing.

Am I, at nearly thirty, becoming the kind of guy that girls find attractive, but whom they write off as actual mating material because my career still earns me less money than most bottle collectors? The question hangs in the air, leaving me unnerved.

When our latest round of Mellonballs arrive, I swoop mine up and take a serious gulp. Holding the glass, I realize my hands are sweating.

Chloe eyes my drink and looks me over, "You okay? You look pale all of a sudden."

I feign a smile and shrug. "I'm great. I was just thinking how nice it'd be to get these to go. Go for a drive. Look at the city lights, something."

Chloe's eyes light up at my suggestion, "That's a great idea! We could go up to Mulholland, maybe park. God, I love you, McGuire. You're always thinking."

God, I love you, McGuire?

The context with which Chloe's just said these words is fairly light, so I do my best to roll it off as an "I love you" in the friendly, I'm a little tipsy vein. I wonder if I'm ever going to learn not to panic when these words are spoken to me, especially by a woman I'm into. After all, they do represent a good thing, for Chrissakes! It's not like she's threatening me with castration.

"Ooh, I know where we can go," Chloe says. "Have you been up to Greystone Mansion?"

I hadn't. I knew of it and had wanted to check it out, but never quite got there.

"It's almost midnight," I say, then ask, "Isn't it closed at night?"

"Well, yes. But if we're quiet and sneak around, I don't think anybody will care, do you?"

I look at her, deciding she's got a point, that some running around in the dark could be fun. It wasn't like U.C.L.A.'s soccer field was a total bust the other night.

"You know how to get up there? To the mansion?" I ask her.

Chloe smiles, nods.

"Should we stop at the liquor store by The Viper Room, grab something to drink?"

Again, Chloe smiles, nods.

I like this girl's attitude.

Except for the moonlighting-in-a-video-store part, that is.

AFTER WE PARK on some neighborhood street north of Sunset in Beverly Hills, Chloe gives me the lowdown on Greystone

Mansion, while the two of us hoof it on foot toward the entrance gates.

Built in the late Nineteen Twenties by some ridiculously rich couple from the area, Greystone Mansion was originally on more than four hundred acres, making it the largest private residence in Beverly Hills. The couple ended up selling it to a wealthy businessman who never actually moved in, and eventually the city of Beverly Hills bought it out and turned it into an historical landmark and park.

Standing in the shadows only a few yards from the gates, Chloe and I peer around, making sure no one is nearby to catch us. With the coast clear, we clutch our bottle of Stoli and make our move, Chloe whispering something about climbing the gate.

Five minutes later Emma Peel and I are on the grounds of this truly impressive structure, the two of us descending a long stone walkway toward the main residence. The night air is cool and only a slight wind blows. With the sky free of clouds, and a three-quarters full moon, Chloe and I are able to move about without any trouble seeing.

"Remember *The Witches Of Eastwick?*" Chloe asks.

"The one with Jack Nicholson and Cher?"

"Uh-huh. They shot a lot of the exteriors here for the castle in the movie," she informs me. "I think Whoopi Goldberg was in another movie here too. Isn't it great?"

Approaching this monster of a house, as we pass by this large, ornate but empty fountain, I nod a yes and mention how cool it would be as a setting for a spooky film.

As if on cue there is a rustle in some bushes not ten feet to our right. For a second I figure we've been nailed by some security guy, or worse, the Beverly Hills P.D., but Chloe tells me of the thousands of squirrels living on the lot, and seeing how no one is calling out for us to stop, I figure a squirrel or another critter is exactly what it is.

I hope so, anyway.

"This place is wild," I say, my eyes going over our surroundings. "How do you know about it?"

"I kind of found it by accident one day, when I first moved out here. I fell in love with it and tried to learn as much about it as possible," she says. Chloe then takes my hand. "I want to show you something."

"You're not setting me up for some kind of satanic sacrifice, are you?"

Chloe pulls me toward the house. "Come on, McGuire."

Not two minutes later, Chloe and I stand at the bottom of a darkened staircase against what is an old, locked wooden door that Chloe claims is where the hired help used to live. There must've been a lot of help, since this part of the mansion is the size of my apartment *complex*.

Our unopened bottle of vodka rests on the ground as we kiss. Chloe unbuttons my pants as I do the same to hers, my hand sliding beneath her panties, her breath coming quickly as I move my hand against her. With two of my fingers inside her, Chloe bites playfully at my lip, then uses a free hand to grab onto my cock, which currently juts out like a goddamned mallet.

"How do you like the mansion?" she asks me between gasps.

"What mansion?"

Pulling one of her pant legs completely off, I lift her up, her back against the wall, and enter her, both of us grinning at each other like . . . well, like two people going at it in a public place in the middle of the night. Working each other into a frenzy, we both sweat like mad dogs in the cool August air.

Again, I hear a rustling, this time somewhere in the bushes above the stairwell.

"I think some squirrels have popped some popcorn and are watching our show," I whisper to Chloe.

"Shut up and fuck me," she says, her hips moving slowly against mine, in perfect sexual rhythm.

Who am I to argue.

Sometime later, in the moments before we both come, Chloe does a little whispering of her own: saying she loves me for what is now, officially, the fourth time since we started hanging out.

I look at her closely, our bodies pressed together hard, and say the only thing that feels right.

I say, "me too."

Yeah, I know, it's not F. Scott Fitzgerald, but I figure it's a decent choice.

SEVEN

Dollars and Scents:

An Oral Examination

"DOES MY VAGINA SMELL LIKE STRAWBERRIES?" Chloe's words hang in the air like L.A. smog, heavily tainting the moment.

I raise my face from between her legs, thrown off by both her question and the suddenness of it. Neither of us says anything for a moment, the radio provides the only sound—The Smith's singing about bigmouth striking again—which, for a second, almost seems appropriate.

"Um," I begin to speak, then wipe my mouth before continuing, "how did we just go from near orgasm to fruit?"

Propping up on her elbows, Chloe gives me this sickly sweet smile. "I only was wondering, if . . . you know . . . if you thought—"

"—your pussy smells like strawberries?" I finish. "Yeah, I got that part. What I'm wondering is *where* this kooky question is coming from?"

Are you sure this is the kind of question you want an answer to?

Chloe shrugs and gives me what should be a considered a

sexy look, but the gesture comes off more like hesitation on her part, like she's stalling while she comes up with an answer.

Or a lie.

"McGuire, it's nothing, really," Chloe sits up and runs her hand across my cheek, her eyes locked on mine. "It was a stupid question. I certainly didn't mean to upset y—"

"I'm not upset."

"And I certainly didn't want you to stop?" Another wannabe sexy smile from her; I can already feel my resolve weakening as she holds her gaze.

I glance down at Chloe's breasts, her belly, then back up to her eyes. "Can I ask you something?"

"Of course."

"Did someone *tell* you that you smelled like strawberries?" I slow my speech for effect and keep my eyes on hers, looking for any signs that might betray her.

Chloe's hand reaches my little friend and gives it a playful squeeze. "Don't be silly."

Oh, well. What the fuck do I know about reading someone's face for deceit, especially when that someone's got my johnson in her clutches? So I decide to edge away from what probably isn't anything other than what she says anyway: a stupid question. Still, I cannot help but try one more angle.

"Lemme ask you something. If you were giving me head and out of the blue I asked you if my schlong tasted like a grilled cheese sandwich, wouldn't you be even a *little* curious as to where that question came from?"

Chloe grins and leans forward, kissing the corner of my mouth. Again her hand finds my now perky side-kick. "McGuire, I told you, it was a stupid question that popped into my head. That's all." Chloe shifts around the bed, now laying on her belly, her eyes filled with a mischievous gleam. "*Does* your schlong taste like a grilled cheese sandwich?"

I want to continue our chat, but with Chloe's face in my lap I decide it can wait.

CHLOE'S STRAWBERRY COMMENT sticks in my mind while

I'm working my shift at Video Schmideo. And because I don't know when to keep my mouth shut, I ask Todd what his thoughts are on the subject. Mistake.

Todd, while cradling a dozen gay pornos, laughs out loud at my predicament, his eyes thin slits as he bellows.

"Thanks, buddy," I say, getting cranky. "Laugh at a man while he's down."

"Terry, you're in this dilemma *because* you went down," he says and walks through the store's main aisle. When his next round of laughing at me mellows, Todd calls out to me from the "Adult" section, "After I shelve these, I'm going next door for a Latte. You want anything?"

Oblivious, I take the bait and say no thanks.

"You sure?" Todd calls back. "Some pie, maybe? Or strawberries and cream?"

There's nothing quite like having your balls busted by a gay man over the subject of pussy.

Maybe I should just ask Isaiah and Drea. They'll probably be more equipped to deal with this subject than Todd.

Hopefully, anyway.

"YOU WANT ME to explain why Chloe's box smells like blueberries?" Drea asks me, her tone already making me regret this little coffee shop pow-wow.

"Strawberries," Isaiah corrects her. "She smells like strawberries."

Drea glances at Isaiah, "Right. Strawberries." She takes a brief drag off her cigarette before turning to me. "You should be glad she smells like fruit. I mean, there are a lot worse things that a woman can—"

"Chloe doesn't smell like any fruit! Not strawberries. Not blueberries. Not goddamned Frankenberries, okay?" I say, a little more impatiently than I intended.

I hate to be short with my friends, but it's a very hot day and A Slug Of Joe's covered patio is doing little to cool us off. The traffic on Sunset is heavy, the smell of exhaust mixing with the scent of fresh coffee. On the patio, in addition to Drea, Isaiah and me, are a dozen wannabe hipsters, striking their poses and sipping their iced coffees and teas.

Drea gives me a brief scowl for rushing her, then pats my hand out of pity. "Well, let's see. If she smells *right* down there, then it wasn't some kind of subtle insecurity coming out."

"She's fine," I assure them. "Really."

"Then it's obvious someone has told her this, that she has a fruit-like quality," Drea explains. "So therefore, the real question is—"

"*When* was she told this?" Isaiah adds flatly.

Drea smiles at our friend, "Exactly. Did some guy say this to her months, or even years ago? Or is this something more recent?" Drea pauses for a moment, glancing at a passing car. "You know I once dated this guy who's cock tasted—"

If she says a grilled cheese sandwich I'm outta here.

"—like a pancake. You know, kind of that doughy—"

Isaiah is laughing as I cut off our man-eating friend. "Drea, let's take this one food item at a time. Please?"

Drea shrugs, takes a drag off her smoke. "Sorry."

"You know what else it could be?" Isaiah begins, his eyes going back and forth between Drea and I. "Chloe could be messing with your head. Wanting you to think that somebody said it, trying to get a reaction."

"Hey, yeah! That's a possibility," Drea says, back into it. "Maybe she's mad, or bummed about some aspect of the relationship, and this is either a test or payback."

I look at my friends, mulling this one over. "You think?"

"You know what they say," Drea answers, "'Hell hath no fury . . .'"

I look at my waif friend, trying to imagine her being so deviant, and ask, "Would you do that to some guy? Fuck with him like that?"

"Would I? No," she says, and adds. "But I'm a remarkable woman who believes too much in karma."

Isaiah, after sipping his iced tea, adds, "And don't forget, Chloe's an actress. So she's extra good at being convincing. At the bullshiting game—"

Drea punches Isaiah's shoulder. "Hey, I'm an actress, too!"

Isaiah gives her a look while rubbing where she hit him. "True, but you're a remarkable woman. You'd never resort to such childish means." He rubs his shoulder some more. "Damn . . ."

I look at my friends some more, unsure. "We do seem to be hitting some sorta relationship . . . *plateau.*"

"So if Chloe did want to screw with your mind, then she's definitely succeeding, the way your obsessing over this," Drea says, mashing out her cigarette with her shoe.

"I'm not *obsessing.*"

"Sweetie, you're ready for a couple blasts of Paxil," she informs me.

I glance down, humbled. Thinking. Wondering how I went from some good old fashioned cunnilingus to being mired in a sexual mystery involving fruit. Maybe Paxil or Prozac isn't such a bad idea.

Shut up, McGuire! Don't be so worried . . .

At the very least, maybe a little time in a monastery would do me some good.

I SIT AT my desk with a Guinness and a bottled water, going over some notes for what will become an outline for my first screenplay. Having decided on a fictitious account of the actual Mulholland Murders (that's what the media have labeled them), I pour over several newspaper clippings, wanting to create a realistic feel to my story.

The phone rings and I let my voice-mail get it.

I stand and move for the phone, irritated that I hadn't turned off the ringer. I decide, since I'm up, to check if a message was left, half hoping it'll be from Chloe.

It's Drea telling me that once I hear this, I need to call her immediately. That she has an idea and wants to run it by me, you know, "get a guy's opinion." I know better, but I dial anyway, curious.

Drea answers her phone on the second ring. When I say hello, she thanks me for calling her back so quickly.

"What's this idea you have?" I ask her.

"Are you thirsty?" Drea asks me in return.

"I'm writing."

"But are you *thirsty*?"

McGuire, you hear it in her voice. She's not giving in . . .

"You don't want to tell me your idea?" I now regret listening to my voice-mail.

"Yes, but I need a drink to do it," she tells me. "Meet me at the Coach and Horse in twenty minutes. No forget it, I'll pick you up in fifteen. Be ready."

"I don't suppose I have a choice in this?"

Drea says nothing for a moment, then asks, "Do you ever?"

THE COACH AND Horse is one of those Hollywood bars that is actually a cool mix of seediness and gloss. It's small, dark and atmospheric: exactly how a bar is supposed to be. Well, almost. You can't smoke inside, which seems strangely backwards for a bar. Then again, this is Los Angeles . . .

We sit at the bar, each with a Tanqueray Tonic in front of us. Drea sips her drink and starts in—finally. She wouldn't discuss her situation until we were in the bar.

"I want to have an intervention for Patrick Friday night. I would've told you today over coffee, but I didn't want to say anything in front of Isaiah. You know, these things are supposed to be fairly discreet."

I look at my friend, unsure of what to say. "I didn't know Patrick was an alcoholic."

Drea sips her T & T, and shakes her head. "He's not."

"What then? Heroin?"

Drea sets her glass on the bar and says, "Good God, no! Nothing so morose." Drea glances at the couple next to us at the bar, and turns back to me before explaining, "He doesn't go down on me."

I look at her, half confused, half wanting to be. "Excuse me?"

"Head? Oral sex? My va-gi-na?" Drea makes a triangle with her fingers on that last one for effect. "He doesn't eat south of the border. At all." Drea looks so utterly serious while she says this I start laughing. Irritated, she takes a long drink off her T & T, finishing it. "It's so frustrating!" she adds, kicking my leg under the bar. "He's such a sweet, smart, sexy guy, that to have this as his one major flaw . . . I don't know if I can go on. It's torture!"

I consider mentioning Patrick's love of his own nose, then decide Drea's plate is already too full with problems.

"Remember our conversation a couple weeks ago? About you giving head to your girlfriends?" she asks.

"Conversation?" I ask, amused. "I remember you grilling me, not much more."

Drea sips from my Tanqueray, makes a cute face at me. "You know what I mean. That night I tried to help Patrick understand that on occasion a woman needs certain, oh fuck it, that women like getting head too! And I guided him down there and he played with me for something like five seconds. Like he was late for work!"

"Did he mention you smelled like strawberries?" I ask, only half kidding, my mind instantly picturing Chloe, my stomach tightening at the memory.

"He was outta there so fast he wouldn't have known!" Drea finishes off my drink. "It's so rude."

"Let me get this straight. You want to have an intervention for him because—"

"Yes!" Drea offers loudly. "A man that doesn't give head is asking for a world of loneliness. And Patrick deserves one last chance to get it together. He'd be perfect if it weren't for this shortcoming."

"I don't know, Drea. This's pretty risky." I tell her. "Guys don't want to be led in any direction sexually, unless they *want* to be led there. I think that made sense . . ."

"I don't have a choice," she says, causing the people next to her to look over. "He'll never figure it out on his own! I have a responsibility to help him see the light."

"Or at least the labia," I add.

Drea gestures at the bartender for another round, then gives me a look. "Come on, sweetie, I need your support on this." She fishes through her bag, pulling out a pack of Marlboro's.

As the bartender brings over fresh T & T's, Drea looks at him, smiling sweetly. "Thanks. By the way, if I light up a cigarette in here, how much is the fine if I refuse to put it out till I'm through?"

Our bartender, this tall guy who's skin is too tan, gives Drea an odd look. "Two hundred and fifty dollars," he tells her and adds, "Plus they ban you from the place."

The latter punishment seems to affect Drea more than the fine; she gives the bartender a less sweet smile this time before turning back to me. "This sucks!" Drea says, while shoving her smokes back into her bag. "I can't have a smoke, and my boyfriend won't eat me out!"

THE NEXT DAY, round about the time most people are getting off work, Chloe and I have just finished getting each other off.

So now we lay in her bed (a spacious King-size), side by side, lying in silence. As the quiet persists, my mind flashes over her strawberry comment, and the fact that while we both still enjoy each other's bodies, I cannot help but admit that the rest of our relationship seems to be losing it's passion. I still look forward to hearing her voice on my voice-mail, but not as much as I used to. And the way Chloe looks at me these last couple weeks, it's as though she's with me more out of habit than desire. As if our time together doesn't carry the same emotional weight.

So bring it up, McGuire. Don't just lay here and stew . . .

"Do you ever think about writing something more than your column in *Angelino Style*?" Chloe asks abruptly, completely derailing my train of thought.

I turn onto my side and look into Chloe's eyes.

"You're a struggling writer who's moonlighting in a video store . . ."

My stomach is tight as I do my best to not come off defensive. "Sure, I do. What makes you ask that?"

"I don't know. I was thinking about how creative you are. That you should keep writing your column because it's a step in the right direction . . ." Chloe's words trail off.

I decide to push it, figuring the can of worms is half open anyway. "And?"

"Well, you've said yourself that the column doesn't pay your bills. Why not try and work on something like a screenplay? Or a novel. Or freelancing on the Internet?" Chloe's voice is soft; there's a hint of hesitancy in her tone, as though she knows this is dangerous ground to tread. Apparently, Chloe doesn't find it too dangerous since she proceeds to tell me that she thinks I'm wasting time working at Video Schmideo, and that I shouldn't be afraid to really commit to my writing, to, "put myself out there."

For a moment I imagine my pop is over Chloe's shoulder, feeding her lines, then admit to myself that this pep talk is all Chloe—even if it is familiar.

"Listen," I start. "I'm not overjoyed at working behind a counter renting out *The Young and the Hung* either, but right now the money's keeping my head above water. It's not a career choice."

"But it is, Terry, in a way. By not investing that time into your writing—into a more ambitious project—you're doing yourself a disservice." Chloe's tone has an unnerving maternal edge to it.

And she's not even calling you McGuire! Now it's Terry . . .

I am now officially defensive and irritated, knowing that in my own man-boy way, anything that pours from my mouth now is going to be laced with attitude.

"Lemme ask you something. How is my working at the video store while pursuing my writing any different than you working at Bloomingdale's while you pursue your acting career?" I ask, trying my best not to sound as annoyed as I feel.

"First of all, you're not doing anything new. You're not trying to move forward, like you're content with the—"

"Chloe, you have no idea what you're talking about," I cut in. "For the past week I've been researching those Mulholland murders, and taking notes on criminal behavior." I pause for a moment, in case she wants to say something, then decide to just keep going, let her yap after I'm through. "Remember that woman they arrested last month? The one who killed those four guys and kept dumping them up on Mulholland? I'm working on a script about that. Kind of a fictional take on it. More about *why* someone becomes a freak like that. *How* they become so detached from society."

When I finally do shut up, Chloe looks at me and says, "Why didn't you tell me about this?"

"You know why," I start in. "Because I don't like talking about what I'm writing until it's either finished or nearly finished. This project is still in the embryotic phase, and I don't want to lose interest in it by babbling about it before I get in deep enough."

Chloe sits up, clearly irritated. "Well, fuck, Terry! How can I support you when you don't even let me in? If you shared this with me, I wouldn't be so . . . *confused* as to where you're mind's at." Chloe turns to face me, her eyes red and tearing up. "You don't give me anything to work with. You don't share anything with me. Not when it comes to what's going on with your life—with our lives! Jesus!" Not waiting for me to do or say anything, Chloe gets up and heads out of her bedroom, telling me she's going to take a shower, that she needs a few minutes to herself.

And there it is.

This entire moment hasn't been brought to you by "Women For Men Who Need Better Careers." This is about me not telling Chloe I love her, plain and simple. This is about the fact that whenever Chloe tries to move us to the next level, I stall like a VW Beetle on a flooded underpass.

Fuck, why am I such a schmuck?

I sit on Chloe's bed, not going after her, unsure as to what I should do.

There isn't a lonelier feeling on Earth than when you and your lover are at odds.

"OF COURSE SHE'S pissed!" Drea tells me as she drives us over to Patrick's apartment the following night. "You can't not respond when a girl says she loves you! You have to say something."

I sigh and take a drag off Drea's cigarette. "I told her 'me too' once."

Drea gives me a look of disgust. "'Me too?' Me too can sound a lot like 'fuck you' if you're not careful. How is it that you have your own relationship column?"

Ah, leave it to Drea to provide support and comfort when it's needed.

"You better be more helpful with Patrick tonight than only spewing out some lazy, simple comments. Remember, you're the only other guy who'll be there, so be ready with some real advice for him. Some genuine oral wisdom." Drea says, taking her cigarette back from me.

"Right. Oral wisdom," I repeat back.

Drea fires another glare my way. "You remember Isaiah and me telling you that Chloe might be testing you with the blueberry comment?"

"Strawberry."

"Whatever," she says, then adds, "You better hope that a test is all it was. Because when a woman begins to lose patience— especially when a guy isn't echoing the same emotions—it all goes downhill fast."

"Yeah, well, it's headed downhill already," I say and shrug. "Believe me."

I take Drea's cigarette from her again, and savor the final drag off it. When I toss the butt out the window, I replay Drea's final words and consider flinging myself out of the car too.

It'd be less painful than dealing with what is most likely to come.

ONE OF THE biggest mistakes a guy can make is giving his house keys to his girlfriend. Even giving them to a simple friend who happens to be a girl can be bad, as my Drea/Wesson encounter taught me all too well.

Patrick also learned this the hard way—about five minutes ago, to be exact—when he entered his place and found four all too familiar people sitting on his couch and leather recliner, each gazing at him with a mixture of annoyance and concern.

Drea, in all her motivated glory, had sniffed out information from Patrick about his last two girlfriends, and then called them up, curious about their thoughts regarding both Patrick and cunnilingus.

Both were all too happy to join in Drea's intervention.

Apparently, Patrick had been running around "headless" for the last few years, leaving more than a couple unsatisfied women in his wake.

Hell hath no fury . . . like a woman denied.

So now, sitting side by side by side on his leather couch, are Amanda, Wendy and Drea, all explaining to our bewildered hero why, if he plans to continue to expect and receive blowjobs, he must learn to reciprocate the favor.

Back up to speed, I sit on the recliner, watching and listening as Patrick is given his just desserts. My mind occasionally flips back to Chloe and our current rocky state, but I do my best to concentrate on the wonderfully wicked scenario before me. I justify staying and witnessing this sit—in in the name of research for my "Sex and the Single Schmuck" column. Not to mention I'd be a fucking idiot to miss something like this.

"Women love getting head," Amanda explains, her tone making her sound like a sex guru slash guidance counselor. "Women enjoy knowing their men like to please them, and head is about as good a way as any." She pauses for a second, then adds, "Well, flowers too. Especially orchids. And roses, of course."

"When a man takes it slow, letting passion dictate the moment, nothing is better," Wendy, this great looking red head, tells Patrick, "than soft, warm lips, and a patiently working tongue."

Jesus, listening to Wendy explain things I have to momentarily picture moldy cheese to keep myself from popping a chubby.

Drea, taking a harder stand, (there's a shock) says to Patrick that most women love to please their man, but that that attitude can quickly fade away if the woman thinks the feeling is less than mutual. This comment makes me think about Chloe and I, and our current state of chaos.

Patrick sits on his living room floor, speechless, perplexed and in disbelief. And probably embarrassed beyond reason, too.

"I know all this seems cruel to you," Wendy says to her ex.

"But think how we feel!" Drea says, jumping in with both feet. "I mean, come on! We're healthy, red-blooded, liberated women. Don't you think we deserve to have our pussies eaten?"

Patrick appears to be shrinking before us, as though the shag carpet beneath him is slowly absorbing him a few centimeters at a time. He looks at me, desperation in his eyes, as if to say "Help me out, buddy."

Drea, catching this, speaks up. "Terry's here, Patrick, to give you a man's perspective on why giving head is good for your love life. I figure since Terry has a column about sex, who better than he to work with you." Drea and the girls all look at me. Drea then instructs me to offer Patrick some advice.

I want to say something constructive, something genuinely helpful. But when I look at him all I can picture is our evening over sushi.

"Well," I start, knowing I'm about to drop the ball. "It's bad enough you don't give head, but you gotta knock off that nose digging shit! You're like a fourth grader!"

The room is painfully silent. Maybe I should get back to the main topic . . . .

OVER THE NEXT two weeks, Chloe and I see less and less of each other. It's like we've started pulling away, not wanting to admit what's happening, but also not fighting it too much either. When we do see each other, the intensity is gone, our time feeling as though Chloe and I are simply going through the motions.

I miss her.

I miss the talking, the fun, the sex. I hate that I haven't heard her laugh in days.

I want to work things out, but know in my gut that by not communicating certain emotions, an instant void was created.

And like a healthy body invaded by cancer, our relationship has begun to break down, our time together slowly, steadily, deteriorating.

I don't know how to fix it.

Yes, I could now start saying I love her, and working harder at being less defensive, and more "boyfriend like." Except at this point, it would all feel forced. Chloe would see it merely as desperation on my part, and that is something I'm not ready to behave like.

Even if desperation *is* what I'm feeling.

BREAKING UP IS more than hard to do, it's a fucking nightmare. It doesn't matter if it's you doing the breaking up, or if you're the one being broken up with, it all still stinks.

And hurts like hell.

Chloe stands in my doorway, her dark eyes full of gloom as

she speaks. "I can't do this anymore, Terry. I know it might seem stupid to you, but when I tell someone I love them, I really want to hear it back. If I don't, it's like I automatically pull away. I really tried with you not to do that, but you're so guarded at times."

I stand there, my feet feeling like fifty pound weights. I want to say so many things, but all that comes out is, "It's not stupid."

Chloe looks at me, her voice a little shaky. "No, but clearly it's not something you're ready to hear, either. I see it in your eyes. It's like you want to run in the opposite direction."

"I'm not that bad—"

"Yes, you are. Even when we were at Greystone and it was dark out, I could feel you tense up when I said I loved you. Like you couldn't wait to get out of there."

I think about that night, about the two of us having sex. I smile at Chloe and tell her that I was tense for more obvious reasons. She barely smiles, not even the corners of her mouth rise. Looking at her, I know she's right, but I still want to hold her anyway. I take a step toward her, my legs feeling heavy, cement like.

"No, don't," Chloe says, holding her hand up. "I'm going to go. I'll call you later. I want some time right now. Some time to think."

I begin to reach for her anyway, telling her not to leave like this, that she knows how much I care about her.

"You're right, Terry. I do know," Chloe says, her eyes getting teary. "That's why I need to take some time away from you."

FIVE MINUTES AFTER Chloe has left, I'm still standing in my front doorway, feeling like the world's biggest jackass. Like a guy that loses a winning lottery ticket—and realizes he might've done it on purpose . . . .

I feel shaky, wanting to scream, cry, drink a keg of Guinness, something.

Anything.

I'm not sure how I get to it, but when I pick up the phone, I immediately call Isaiah at work. He tells me that he's got a few more patients and that he'll call me back a.s.a.p. Isaiah then advises me to relax and not to beat myself down. Before we hang up, he also says that I should call Drea.

DREA AND I sit on my patio, Drea holding my hands in hers. I tell her everything, fighting off the need to ball like a school boy. Drea hugs me closely, saying that it's going to take some time, that Chloe has to do what's best for herself, and that I do too.

"You know the lamest part?" I say, looking at my friend. "Once Chloe stopped calling me McGuire, and started calling me Terry, I knew we were in trouble."

"Chloe's looking for something that right now you're not, that's all," Drea says, then adds, "but you're wrong about what the lamest part is."

I look at my friend, unsure.

"Now you may never know what her blueberry comment was about," she offers.

"Strawberry."

"Whatever," she says, then gives me a smile and bumps against me affectionately.

Though I still feel like shit, I love Drea for trying to lighten things up—for her effort.

As we sit together, I realize that when everything else is swirling the bowl, you can always fall back on your friends. And even if they fumble the catch, the true ones will be there—no matter what— to help you get back up.

EIGHT

An Early Fall

THE LAST TWO WEEKS HAVE BEEN FILLED with the advice of others. Only now, as I start to emerge from my fog of depression, do I realize how varied (not to mention, scary) some of the advice has been.

Drea said to take some time for myself and to allow Chloe the same courtesy. She also made me promise to never try to "help" her with another intervention.

Isaiah said basically the same thing (minus the intervention stuff), and told me to make sure I didn't beat myself up about my choices concerning the L-word. That too many people throw around "love" too easily.

Scotty brought up the Internet, and how easy it'd be for him to set us up on a blind slash double date, and that the girls wouldn't be skanky.

My Grandma Kate told me that everything happens for a reason, and to work on my writing. She also offered to send me a box of sugar cookies.

My pop told me to come up for a visit, that a few rounds of golf can cure most anything. He also said to talk to mom about my feelings, to not be afraid to do it, or to feel strange about it.

Our Poker buddy, Pete, warned me not to listen to anything Scotty might say, and that if I wanted to call Chloe, I should do it, but not to force anything.

My sis, Tricia, offered her place for a few days if I wanted a change of setting, and told me to use the experience with Chloe in my writing, in my column.

Sabrina called out of the blue, and after giving her the lowdown, she offered to take me out for dinner—someplace where all the food was fresh.

Todd at Video Schmideo said I should swear off women for six months and come hang with him and his friends at Rage—this gay bar in West Hollywood—that his friends would provide an "interesting perspective."

Sitting here, working on my column for the November issue, I wish mom was around. I wonder what her advice would be. I think about my pop, and how, since mom's death, he has immersed himself in golf, learning the craft and working at it. Though Chloe's and my break-up isn't anywhere nearly as serious as mom's cancer, I decide that I need the same kind of outlook. Like my sis and grandma said, I should use all that has happened and channel it into the writing. At worst, I'll have some stories to throw onto the *Angelino Style* fire.

The Miles Davis's "Sketches In Spain" disc ends, catching my attention. I get up and reach for Neil Young's "Harvest," my brain switching over to my still in-limbo screenplay about the Mulholland Murders. Yes, this is definitely the time to concentrate on my writing. You know how many writers go for months without a thought in their head? Here I am, a regular column in a Los Angeles magazine, and a solid script idea.

So stop thinking about 'em and get to work . . .

The telephone rings as Neil Young's voice pours from the speakers. Since I'm up, I figure I'll answer it; it could be something important. Or someone important.

It could be Chloe.

I grab the phone and say, "Hello?"

"I'm an hour away from finishing up at the office, and I feel like having a drink," Isaiah declares. "I'm thinking you ought to join me, end this hermit lifestyle you've been livin'."

I look at my half-completed column and think about my script, knowing what I need to do, knowing it's time to buckle down and—

"Okay, I'll go," I tell him.

Apparently, Isaiah was expecting me to put up a fight, because he starts in on a rant about how I need to spend more time with my friends.

"Isaiah?" I interrupt. "I said I'll go."

There is a pause on the other end, Isaiah then says, "Good man. About—fucking—time you came outta that cave."

We hang up. The guilty side of me forces me to look at the column on my makeshift desk. Fuck it, it'll still be there in a few hours. Actually, at the pace I'm moving these days, it'll still be there in a few weeks.

LOLA'S ON FAIRFAX is good for a few different things: tasty Macaroni and Cheese, great green-apple Martini's, and excellent eye candy.

It's barely seven-thirty, and while the place is far from packed, there is still a cozy number of people pouring back drinks and checking each other out.

Isaiah and I sit on a couple stools at the bar, drinking Martinis and quietly chatting. Isaiah finishes telling me about a client of his who was in a nasty car accident, that left his spine resembling a large pretzel.

Then, for a moment, the two of us sit quietly, each nursing our own drink.

Each in our own little world.

Naturally my thoughts turn to Chloe, to what she might be up to right about now. It's not so much a specific thing I'm wondering, but more of a glum feeling, like six weeks ago we were inseparable and now I'm in a bar . . . wondering what it is she might be doing. Without me . . . .

Over the speakers, R.E.M.'s "Sad Professor" plays, Michael Stipe singing about hating where he's wound up.

"How're you doing, Terry?" Isaiah asks me.

I look at him, seeing the sincerity in his eyes. "I'm cool. Taking it day by day."

Isaiah sips his drink, then asks me how long he and I have known each other.

"Jesus," I start, "four, nearly five years." I look at him, curious, "Why?"

A tall, and very leggy brunette passes by, momentarily shaking our attention. Isaiah mumbles something about loving L.A. and then has another sip of his green apple Martini before directing his focus back on me.

"You're not beating yourself up too much, are you? 'Bout you and Chloe falling through?"

I sip my drink, a sliver of ice sliding down my throat, and shake my head at him. "I don't think so. Not any more than usual . . . ." I pause, deciding honesty is key to any friendship. "Well, yeah, a little more than usual. But that's because I liked her a lot more than most of the girls I've dated."

"I understand that. That makes sense. But what I want you to understand is it's not your fault," he says, his comment surprising me. "*Any* of it."

I study Isaiah closely, fairly sure as to what he's talking about. I ask anyway, "You mean about Chloe and me, or about my mom dying?"

"I mean *all* of it," he says, and then goes into this Sigmund Fraud ramble. "You were a kid, Terry! I hope you see that. I hope you realize you don't need to punish yourself. That it's okay for you to get close to Chloe, or whoever it is you're da—"

"Okay, you know what? Let's not do this right now." I interrupt, thrown off by Isaiah's candor. "Not now."

Isaiah holds up a hand and nods. "All I'm saying is you ought to start giving yourself credit. Cut yourself some slack. Not everything that happens to you is your fault." Isaiah pauses for a moment, only long enough for me to notice that my heartbeat is speeding up. "Think about it, that's all. You have it good, man. And I don't think you let yourself realize it."

Irritated, I finish the rest of my drink and give Isaiah a look. I want to remind him that my girlfriend dumped me because I wouldn't commit. I want to remind him that I currently have seventy-nine dollars in my checking account. I want to remind him that as far as my career goes, I barely have a career going. I want to remind him it's fucked up losing a parent. Knowing my mom can never call me on the phone. That she cannot ever be there for Christmas, or my sister's birthday, or anything, ever again.

Instead, I say nothing for a few moments, and then flag down the bartender and order us two more drinks.

AROUND MIDNIGHT, WHILE working on my column and listening to Billie Holiday, my thoughts drift back to what Isaiah said earlier at Lola's. Could he be right? Have I become so accustomed to having no money, only short term-relationships, and an identity as the-struggling-writer-whose-mom-died-when-he-was-a-kid, that I've become afraid to actually allow myself to succeed? Have I become so paralyzed by my own whining and narcissism, that enjoying what I *do have* is no longer possible?

The questions leave me unsettled. I look at my monitor, at the words before me, and begin typing with a sense of urgency.

Billie Holiday continues to sing as I work my keyboard like a man-boy possessed.

"GUYS ARE PATHETIC!" Isaiah says with disdain.

Scotty gives him a couple looks, apparently trying to make sure Isaiah's comment isn't personally directed at him.

The three of us run the Hollywood Reservoir in the late morning, the air cooler than usual for early October. Bolting in front of us, as we continue our chat slash run, a squirrel does a hard left, then jigs back to it's right, clearly wanting to avoid our presence.

"I'm telling you what she told me! She read it in some chick magazine." Scotty explains, referring to his latest girlfriend, Betsy, who has clearly put the sexual pressure (not to mention the fear of God) on our friend by telling him that the average length of time a man lasts during sex—from insertion to orgasm—is barely six minutes. According to Scotty J, Betsy threatened that if he didn't (or couldn't) improve upon this sad average by leaps and bounds, she'd find a man that could.

"It's not like what she's asking is so tough, it's the fact that she even brought it up," he continues, his breath coming harder the more he yaps. "I'd have never thought about it on my own. But now, I'm freaked I might crumble under the pressure."

"You sure 'crumble' is the word you mean?" I ask.

"So now she's always bringing up the six-minute factor," Scotty says.

Isaiah looks at him, not getting it. "What do you mean, six minute fac—"

"Like I said about the sex stuff! Betsy's always putting weird comments out there, like, 'Did you know a rerun of *Seinfeld* is five times longer than the average sexual encounter?' Or she'll tell me, after we're done boning, I lasted nine and a half minutes. Like she's clocking me for the Olympics or something." Scotty stops running, his breathing harsh, clearly bothered by all of this.

Isaiah and I look at each other, then also stop running. Scotty, his hands on his thighs, looks as though he might vomit.

"You okay?" I ask, fairly irritated that we've stopped before the first mile mark.

Scotty gives us a weak wave, and stands up, his face red. "I can't run . . . and talk this fast . . ."

"You gotta cut out those cheap cigars, Scott," Isaiah advises. "Shit's bad for you."

Scotty gives another wave, says he's gonna rest, and for us to keep running, that he'll meet us back at my Cherokee.

"Come on, Janwankowski, let's get going!" I order. "We've run this fucker a thousand times!"

Scotty sits down on the path, his breathing still hard. "Dude, I'm tired, gimme a break!" He then lays down on the course, and mumbles about Betsy's six minute comment messing with his head.

I glance at Isaiah's watch, seeing that we've been running barely five minutes. Irritated, I look at our drained friend lying on the course. "It happens to everyone, Scotty. Don't sweat it so much."

"Never happens to me!" Isaiah pops off.

"Shut up, tough guy," I say, giving Isaiah a look. "I'm trying to be supportive, here. Get our boy off the ground, and start running." I turn back to Scotty. "Come on, Scotty J! Let's do this thing together. We'll take it slow."

"Nah, go ahead without me. I'll meet you at the Jeep." Scotty sits up and gives us another fucking wave.

Officially cranky, I look from Isaiah's watch and back to Scotty, shouting out, "How the hell do you expect to fuck for more than six minutes, when you can't even *run* that long?"

Scotty give me the finger while Isaiah lets out a laugh.

"Nice. Very supportive, Terry," Isaiah offers. He then adds, "You wanna kick him in the leg too?"

OUR THREE POINT two mile run complete, Isaiah and I do some stretching, neither of us wanting to cramp up. A hundred feet up the street, where joggers park their cars, I spot Scotty leaning against my Cherokee, talking to some tall, thin girl, her light hair in a ponytail.

"Look at him, Isaiah," I say, pointing toward our knucklehead friend. "He's too tired to run with us, but still has the energy to try and get laid." I pause for a second, and watch as he and the girl laugh over whatever it is they're talking about. "If he gets her phone number, I'm gonna bust his schnoz."

"Forget it. Scott'll blow his wad too fast, and he'll never see her again." Isaiah says.

After a few more stretches, Isaiah and I make our way toward the car. Isaiah then brings up the other night, his comments at Lola's. "Life's hard enough as it is. No reason for you to keep yourself at a greater disadvantage," he tells me, then adds, "I didn't want to lecture you, and that's exactly what I ended up doing."

Knowing this is Isaiah's way of smoothing out any possible tension, I smack him on the shoulder and tell him he is right, that I'm so busy complicating things and whining about them, I never really learn to appreciate what's good around me.

I suddenly think about Chloe, her face clear in my mind, her great, dark eyes. I wonder what she's up to as Isaiah and I walk. I wonder if she's at work, or maybe out with friends, maybe some guy she's met recently. Not happy with the last possibility, I shake off the thought and stare up the pathway.

Twenty feet from the Cherokee, Isaiah and me watch Scotty and Miss Ponytail shake hands and *hug*, this singular act causing Isaiah and me to gape at each other with equal parts disbelief and envy.

"Oh, he's dead," I say, checking out the girl as she heads toward her own car.

Isaiah, still sweating from our three point two mile run, wipes at his slick forehead and eyes Scotty, "I'll hold him down while you beat his ass . . ."

ONE OF THE scarier things about being an adult (technically, anyway) is the fact that the more independent you become, the more you become indebted to everyone else, as in the gas company, the electric company, the phone company, and so on.

So when Todd called me, wondering if I wanted to pull a "double" at Video Schmideo this morning, all I had to do was look at my growing stack of bills before I said yes. What else was I going to do? I had finally finished next month's column the night before, Chloe and I were dead in the water, and I knew both Drea and Isaiah were at work themselves. Besides, when it was slow at the video store, I could continue my outline for the Mulholland Murders script.

So now, three hours into my twelve hour work day, I stand in the Horror section with an inquisitive yet knowledgeable customer. The customer, a portly girl with three rings in her left nostril, is actually pretty cool, her taste in movies leaning towards the quirky side. As we talk, she goes on about how she recently finished up her directorial debut, a twelve minute short film about a group of mutated lesbians that live in the sewers beneath West Hollywood. She tells me the short is going to be shown at this year's Lesbian Cinema Festival, which is happening at the end of this month, a couple days before Halloween. When she mentions that she also wrote the script for her film, I decide that maybe I was meant to meet this girl today, that maybe it would be a good thing to get to know some of my creative peers. Multiple nose rings or not.

Extending my hand, I introduce myself and congratulate her on completing what is a serious achievement.

The girl shakes my hand and smiles widely, exposing two piercing studs in her tongue. "I'm Pilar. I've seen you working here before, but only a couple of times."

"Yeah, Todd, the owner, takes pity on me when he sees I'm in need of real work. So I accept his charity whenever possible," I explain, not the least bit embarrassed by the truth of my words.

Standing here, talking to Pilar, this total stranger, I can't help but find it ironic that I feel totally at ease admitting my need for extra cash, yet when Chloe would bring it up I would instantly become defensive. It doesn't make a lot of sense, but it is what it is. Maybe—probably—there was more at stake with Chloe.

Pilar pulls *The Exorcist* and *Angel Heart* off the shelves, and holds them up, explaining how she's in the mood for "some quality time with the devil."

"Well, you can't go wrong with either," I agree. "And if you're still hungry after those, you can always grab *The Omen*. Spend time with Satan as a kid."

"I've seen that one pretty recently," Pilar tells me as she scans over the *Angel Heart* video box. She then looks at me, making direct eye contact as she asks, "So when you're not helping out here, what do you do?"

"Well, to a certain degree, I'm a writer," I say.

She smiles a little and asks, "To a *certain* degree?"

Don't be such a sissy, McGuire! You're a writer, you don't have to play it down.

"No, I'm an actual writer. I just hate saying it in a town where everyone and their mother says the same thing," I babble. "I feel like I sound flaky, saying it sometimes."

Pilar nods in understanding. "It's only flaky if you're *not* writing."

Ding-ding! Now that makes sense.

I smile at her as we walk out of Horror and toward the counter. "That's true. I should remind myself of that more often."

Pilar hands me her movies and gives me a friendly look. "Yes, you should."

Once I've scanned and bagged her movies, I hand them to her and we exchange "nice to meet yous." As she is about to exit, Pilar turns back and mentions that next time she's in, she'll bring me a flyer for the Lesbian Cinema Festival, and that if I'm interested, I should check out her short film.

To my surprise, as she says this, Scotty J walks in, giving me a nod.

"That'd be great," I tell Pilar. "If I'm not here, tell whoever is to tape the flyer to my time card."

Pilar and her piercings give me a final smile before exiting, leaving Scotty and I alone—except for the old guy "loitering" in the Adult section.

"Who was that?" Scotty asks me, referring to Pilar.

"This cool girl who's got a movie in an upcoming festival," I tell him, and then add dryly, "You know, Scotty? If I wasn't convinced she's a lesbian, I'd say she was hitting on me."

"No dude, she was too fat," Scotty says, with his usual dose of tact. "I know you're still messed up over Chloe, but trust me, you can do better."

I consider spelling things out for my semi socially-retarded friend, that I was kidding about Pilar actually hitting on me, but then figure I'll just move on and see what brings him in.

Scotty hedges a bit in answering my question, and then glances around the store.

"We're empty," I say. "'Cept for Grandpa Moses checking out the gay porn."

After hesitating a bit more, Scotty finally starts in, his voice quiet. "It happened."

I look at him, unsure. "What happened?"

Scotty clears his throat and leans toward me a little as he speaks. "Remember yesterday, I was telling you about Betsy giving me all that shit about keeping it up?"

I nod, already knowing where this one's headed. "The six-minute factor?"

"Uh, huh. We were boning last night and it happened," he says, his face full of worry. "I blew my load too quick, dude. *Way* too quick."

I stand there, not a hundred percent sure how to respond to this. But I see that Scotty's frustrated and embarrassed, so I refrain from making any smart-assed comments. For the moment, anyway.

"Well, like I said yesterday, it happens. You just have to look at it as the occasional misfire, you know? Like when someone's at the firing range and their gun goes off before they aim at the target." I shrug and pat him on the shoulder. "How'd Betsy react?"

Now Scotty shrugs, and makes a face. "She said she was

flattered, but I could tell she was bugged. I'm afraid now that I'm so worked up about this, it's gonna keep happening. Like my dick's betraying me!"

The truth is, coming too fast happens to guys all the time. It's like speeding on the freeway . . . sometimes you just can't help yourself. The first time I had sex, I lasted less time than it would take you to hear about the new, improved Whopper from Burger King. Even as recently as when Chloe and I were disintegrating, my performance suffered heavily, making me feel like that much more of a jackass.

The trick, I think, is to not stress out about it. To think about other things while you're having sex. From baseball to fly fishing. From bad Sylvester Stallone movies to your golf swing. Roadkill to Strom Thurman. Long as your brain isn't focused totally on where your willy is, you should be A-O-Kay.

Of course, that's easier said than done . . . .

"I thought, since you have your column, you might have some ideas about how to keep this from happening again," Scotty says to me, his tone hopeful.

After several seconds of thinking, and an entire mental reel of unappealing images, I decide on one specific visual that should truly help my friend keep his demanding girl happy, and his fragile ego intact.

I walk around the counter and lead my anxiety-ridden friend down the store's main aisle, talking as we go. "Scotty, I want you to soak up what you're about to see. Really take it in, and the next time your schlong is ready to . . . well, you know . . . just remember this particular image, and you shouldn't have any trouble."

Scotty gives me an optimistic smile, sensing that the promise of a return to manhood is within his sights.

As we walk I can hear the slightest of groans from the other side of the wall, which tells me our timing is perfect. And with that, we turn the corner into Video Schmideo's Adult section and find our oldest and most loyal customer, whipping his ancient skippy while clutching what is apparently his video box cover "pick" of the day.

Judging by Scotty's reaction—and the mortified look plastered on his face—he'll never need another image to keep himself from falling short of the dreaded six-minute mark.

Then again, if Scotty replays this moment in his mind too much, he could have a problem with impotency.

Of course, there is Viagra for that . . . .

YOU WOULD THINK that twelve hours of clerking at a video store, helping Scotty J with his quick-trigger crisis, and dealing with an old queen that masturbates to porn covers would have worn me out. Instead, I sit on my living room floor working on the characters for my first feature length screenplay. With papers spread about me and several photocopies of newspaper articles on my lap, I think about Chloe; where she might be right now, and who she might be out with.

Bryan Ferry is on the stereo, the hipster crooner singing about boys and girls.

The thoughts I have for Chloe are less and less jealous, or insecure, but more and more of simple wonder. Sure I miss her, and at times I wish I had just given in and said what she wanted to hear. But now, for the first time, I am feeling okay about us splitting up. I'm okay with the fact that, as Drea put it, Chloe and I were at two different places, looking for two different things.

I sit there, taking a sip off my Guinness, knowing that no matter what, there are always going to be guys out there better than me—more suited for relationships in the traditional sense of the word. And while that is a fact, I also know that there is no other guy in town quite like me. For better or worse, warts and all, I still do have something to offer, even if I spend half my time trying to figure out what that something is.

My mind drifts to Mom, and how shitty it is to see someone pass through her life ahead of schedule. I picture her last few days, how even when her physical strength was gone, she was still my sister's and my *mom*; telling us what to do, how to behave. One of the last things mom told me was to not waste time, to not take my life for granted.

I was sixteen when she told me that.

I think now, as I edge toward thirty, it's time to finally listen and take her advice.

NINE

I, Candy

EDITORIAL ASSISTANT JANE BYRON CALLS, sounding concerned as she asks me if everything is all right.

For more than a year, whenever I've had a question, complaint or problem, Jane's been the woman to see over at *Angelino Style*; her no-nonsense attitude is great, and her ability to always remain diplomatic is even better. So it feels strange to hear her sound more like a mother than an editorial assistant.

"Yeah, I'm doing o-kay," I say, giving the "okay" extra oomph. "What's up?"

"Well, Susan and I were going over your column this morning, and both of us came away from it feeling fairly glum. You've tackled dark subjects before, but always with a sense of humor," Jane explains, her tone even, diplomatic. "To be honest, Terry, this story hasn't an ounce of humor in it. Your pieces are meant to be fun and light, and this particular column isn't. At all."

Jane is right; my latest column is all about the woes of breaking up, the inspiration coming from my own "Chloe experience," and the neurosis that ensued.

"I know it's less than happy, but I think it's important to mix it up a bit. By writing only light, playful columns all the time, I haven't allowed for any depth. But now, with an article like this one, readers will be . . . *thrown*, hopefully making them pay closer attention to 'Sex and the Single Schmuck,' as well as the magazine as a whole! Not to mention, the next humorous article will come off that much more funny, by comparison." With the bullshit meter off the charts, I still manage to find some logic and honesty in what I've just said.

Yeah . . .

Jane takes a moment before asking the obvious, "You do understand this column is to be included in the November issue?"

I stare into my fishless aquarium, watching the bubbles on top of the filtered water. "Yes?"

"Well, Terry, we like our November issue—our pre *holiday* issue—to set the tone for the season. Chanukah? Christmas? This is when the magazine's overall energy needs to be, well . . . *festive.*" I can feel Jane churning out the diplomacy as she continues. "But this particular 'Sex and the Single Schmuck' is not festive. It isn't going to make the reader laugh. It isn't going to make the reader feel cozy, or even smile. It's only going to make the reader want to slit his or her wrists!"

"So you're saying were it not the season to be jolly, this article would be acceptable?" I don't like asking Jane a question this heavy with attitude, but it comes out anyway.

As she did earlier, Jane takes a moment before answering. "I'm saying . . . I'm *asking* you, for the first time, to please re-write your column."

I sense Jane's anxiety and censor the half dozen or so comments that have popped into my head. I know this is tougher on her to ask than it is for me to hear.

"You know how much we love your stuff around here, Terry," she adds. "Think of something that has a theme in keeping with the time of year, that's all. Think about Thanksgiving. The holidays. Remember, we're shooting for festive."

Respecting Jane too much to argue (and needing the gig even more), I tell her I'll brainstorm and call her in the morning with something. I then say how much I appreciate her honesty and straightforwardness.

Don't forget her diplomacy.

We hang up and I plop onto my couch, where I begin panicking. Something about relationships that's in keeping with the holiday season?

I could always write about the percentage of farmers that fuck their turkeys.

I'm not sure that fits the festive mold.

And why the hell do I have to be the "fun, light" guy at *Angelino Style*? Why can't I be the dark, brooding guy?

Festive!

What a crock.

I get up and walk into the bedroom, checking out my *Raiders of the Lost Ark* poster, wondering what Indiana Jones would do in my position. And while I realize the silliness of my question, I get the sneaking suspicion Indy would never allow himself to get into this situation in the first place.

A wise man, he is.

As far as fictional characters go, anyway.

DREA STOPS BY, a couple of catalogs in her hand. Following her into my bathroom, I watch in fascination as she places a *Pottery Barn* and *J. Crew* on the back of the toilet, slid just beneath my current *Rolling Stone*. Drea explains that when girls spot these catalogs, they'll see me as the kind of guy that pays attention to what's hip and fashionable when it comes to my garb and home. She glances at the black soap dish and picture frame she brought me, both still in their originally placed positions. In the picture frame is an old shot of my pop and I playing the links. Drea nods in approval of my choice.

"What're you hungry for?" Drea asks, now heading for my bedroom.

"Doesn't matter. Any food will do, except Thai," I say, shrugging. "I'm not in the mood for Thai."

Drea surveys my bedroom, her eyes coming to rest on my still-puny bed. Saying nothing, she simply shakes her head.

"You know what sounds good?" I ask, trying to divert her attention. "Sea food."

Drea turns and gives me a nod. "That *does* sound good. But we're still discussing your bed while we eat."

AT THE REEL Inn in Malibu, Drea and I share a basket of fish
and chips and a bucket of clams. Sipping on a Coke, I listen as
Drea tells me about a party on Halloween she wants us to go to,
where Ecstasy will allegedly be given out free at the front door.

"And Halloween candy, of course," she adds, smiling. "Last
year was a blast!"

We each work on a clam before Drea asks me why I wasn't
with her last Halloween.

"Last Halloween?" I muse, trying to recall. Then I remember
the reason, which is painfully unexciting. "Oh, I know. I had some
kind of stomach virus, flu thing."

"That's right, you did! I brought you a pumpkin, didn't I?"
Drea asks.

"Yes. Yes, you did. That was very cool."

I smile at the thought, the memory. I'd gotten horrifically sick
the day before Halloween. When I wasn't flat on my back in bed, I
was flat on my ass on the toilet—as only the flu can do. Drea and
her friend Lyndsy had dropped by on their way to drinking and
debauchery, and set me up with a few horror videos and a carved
pumpkin, complete with a burning candle inside. And as a result,
despite my dilapidated state, I was still able to enjoy the feel of
Halloween.

Even as I dehydrated faster than a frog in the desert.

"Well, sweetie, we'll make sure you have fun this year," Drea
tells me as she clinks her soda glass against mine.

Sitting here with Drea, looking at her and thinking about her
bringing me the pumpkin, I wonder why she and I have never
hooked up. We're very flirty with one another. We tell each other
intimate things the rest of the world is fairly clueless about. We
even agreed (under the severe influence of booze) to marry each
other if no one else came along by the time we were both thirty-
five. 'Course, the idea of marriage is . . .

"Do you think I'm a decent catch?" I ask, knowing my query is
out of the blue.

Drea washes down another clam before answering. "You mean
as a boyfriend?"

I nod a yes, hoping her answer is both honest and good for my ego.

What're you kidding? This's Drea! The answer will be honest. Whether you like it or not is another thing . . .

"Oh, sweetie, you know you are!"

God bless Drea. My ego is—

"You're a neurotic mess, but you're a mess in the best kind of a way," she adds.

—not quite sure how to take this.

A neurotic mess?!

I must be frowning or look discouraged, because Drea gives me this wildly cute crooked grin and says not to wig out, that she still loves me to death.

I want to ask her to elaborate, and then decide against it, changing the subject to the lesbian film festival we're attending tonight instead.

"I can't wait," Drea says, then asks me, "How'd you meet this girl? Pilar, is it?"

"She rents from Video Schmideo, and one day we just started hitting it off," I explain. "She brought in a flyer for this thing tonight, and we've been talking a lot about writing and movies." I pause and take a bite of the Cod. "It's funny. I know she's gay, but I swear it feels like she's hitting on me half the time."

Drea gives me a funky look and asks, "She a lesbian, though, right?"

"Yeah," I say. "Yeah, I mean . . . yeah."

Another funny look from Drea before she pulls her cigarettes from her bag and says, "See, this's what I mean, Terry. You think you're the object of some lesbian's affection. This's in perfect keeping with you being neurotic." Drea pulls out one smoke and glances at it before continuing. "You're lucky you're as cute and charming as you are. Insecurity and narcissism don't usually look good on people."

I watch Drea for a moment, my defenses growing. I want to argue, but take another bite of Cod instead, knowing I can't say anything too lame with a mouthful of fish.

PILAR'S SHORT FILM is easily one of the best of the night.

Drea and I, along with a couple hundred other folks, sit through a dozen films, Pilar's getting the most laughs, which is a good thing, since it is a comedy.

Afterwards, amidst the other attendees showering Pilar with accolades, Drea and I give her a quick hello and a thumbs up, expecting to slip out quietly, not wanting to tie her up. Instead, Pilar gives me a monster hug and Drea a big kiss on the mouth, clearly wired from the evening's events. The three of us visit for a while, Drea and Pilar hitting it off like two peas in a pod—or two women at a lesbian film festival.

When we finally do head out, Drea advises me to stay in touch with Pilar, that the more talented writers I hang around, the better I'll feel about the entire process, from the creative stuff to my own confidence.

"As long as they're not pretentious, you'll benefit from their company," she says as we drive toward Swingers for a couple Espresso Milkshakes. "And they'll benefit from your company too."

I glance at my friend as she fires up a cigarette, thinking about the question I asked her earlier at the Reel Inn. I didn't even ask if I was a good catch, boyfriend wise. I used the word "decent."

You gotta start feeling better about yourself, McGuire.

Drea looks at me and gives me a smile. With her free hand, she makes a fist and gives me an affectionate slug on my thigh. As she turns to stare out the window, I decide that if she and I do make it to thirty-five and haven't found anyone else to marry, I would be fucking lucky to have Drea as a back up.

Course, between now and then, I need to get over my fear of commitment.

LATER THAT NIGHT, while lying in my bed for one—with Kobe Bryant and Indiana Jones watching over me—I think of what Drea said about keeping company with writers. Would other legitimate writers believe I had something to offer the world? Would they see any talent, or would I be shrugged off as another wannabe? Yes, I have a column in a good sized magazine, and am now ready to write my first feature screenplay, but, in a city where even busboys have penned scripts, would I really have a shot at becoming a serious, successful writer? And would I seem credible?

A few years ago, while I waited tables at Pinot in Hollywood, I got to know this homeless guy who lived in an overturned dumpster near the restaurant. His name was Larry, and even he had a script he carried around with him, something he'd written right before his last bit of sanity slipped away. Thinking about Larry gets my mind racing, my need for sleep dwindling quickly, replaced with a need for work.

Ten minutes later, with Tracy Chapman on the stereo, I begin writing my screenplay, my fingers working the keyboard.

I think about Larry, wherever he is. I hope he's happy, crazy or not.

AS A KID, Halloween was one of my favorite days of the year. It was scary, but in an exciting, bright-eyed way. People opened their doors to you, and you didn't have to worry too much about the consequences. Sure, older kids would tell you stories of apples laced with pins and razor blades, and the occasional neighbor kept his or her mean—ass dog in the front yard, keeping you to the other side of the street while you trick—or—treated. But overall, Halloween was a fun, innocent time, and the candy was plentiful.

When I wake up it is noon, Halloween day.

I stayed up until four this morning, and pumped out the first eleven pages of my as yet untitled screenplay. Yes, I am using the recent Mulholland Murders as my guide, but last night I solidified my decision to let my story be more about people. What makes someone become a serial killer? What do these people do when they're not out committing evil deeds? And do the people in their lives suspect that their friend, or lover, is in fact, spending part of his or her time dumping bodies along a gorgeous stretch of Southern California road?

As I get out of bed, I think about the script and picture myself in a meeting, some Industry goofball listening to me as I pitch the story. "So you see, it's not just your *typical* serial killer movie. It's got heart. It's got brains. It's a serial killer movie that makes you think. It's *the* quintessential thinking person's serial killer movie! Think *Basic Instinct* meets *Crime and Punishment . . .*"

I brush my teeth and splash water on my face, amazed, despite the minimal amount of sleep I got, at how much energy I have. How good I feel.

You see, Terry, this is what a good night's writing will do.

Once I'm dressed, I decide to go for a run around the reservoir, wanting to take full advantage of my current Ginko state. Besides, running always helps me with my writing. You wouldn't believe how many ideas and creative juices seep out over the course of three point two miles. Not to mention the fact that it is Halloween, and I have every intention of having fun tonight—that fun including drink and whatever else—which means it may be a few days before I get another run in.

Dressed and heading for my Cherokee, I see a huge U-haul in front of the complex. My occasionally too loud next door neighbor is moving out. I watch for a minute as he and a couple buddies maneuver his couch into the truck. It's funny, I lived next to this guy for the past two years and I haven't a clue what his name is. All I know is there were some days when I wanted to put a muzzle on him, mainly due to his tendency to sing slash bellow in the shower at eight a.m. And now that he's leaving for wherever, I feel like a schmuck for not at least trying to know him.

Remember what mom said, about not wasting time . . .

Maybe I'll meet the next person who moves in. Maybe he or she will be cool, the kind of neighbor you spend a night beside the complex pool with, yapping and sharing a bottle of wine, or a couple of beers.

In the meantime, I give my now former neighbor a final glance, and get in my car. It's Halloween, and before I party with both girls and ghouls, I want to take a run. Seems like the healthy thing to do.

ISAIAH HAS LEFT me a message saying he and this cutie he's seeing will be meeting Drea and I at the party tonight, that they'll be dressed as the original John Shaft and Foxy Brown.

Drea and Lyndsy, already sounding tipsy, are at Drea's getting their costumes together; the message they leave goes on for a full two minutes.

I sit around the kitchen for a minute, wondering what, or who, I should be tonight.

And then it hits me.

Ernest Hemingway was born in Illinois on July Twenty First, Eighteen Ninety Nine. By the age of eighteen he was a reporter for the *Kansas City Star*. He had written and published *The Sun Also Rises* by the age of Twenty Seven. Hemingway would go on to write *A Farewell To Arms*, *To Have and Have Not*, and, of course, *The Old Man and the Sea*, a novel that would earn him the Nobel Peace Prize for Literature in Nineteen Fifty Four. He would also become a raging alcoholic, who battled liver disease, diabetes, and severe depression. In the end, one of America's greatest, and most respected writers, Ernest Miller Hemingway, would kill himself.

So now, I, Terry McGuire, one of L. A.'s least known, and barely respected writers, will become him. Ernest Hemingway, for a night. For Halloween.

It's better than going as myself.

THE HALLOWEEN PARTY is at an apartment located in the Miracle Mile, near the La Brea Tar Pits, the "miracle" apparently being if you're able to find a parking place.

Inside the Twenties-style building, a few dozen guests—most of whom are in costumes-drink, flirt and trip on whatever substances flow through their bloodstreams.

No Ecstasy is passed out at the front door, but someone dressed as Tipper Gore gives Drea, Lyndsy and I each a big smooch on the lips as we enter.

Drea looks fucking great. She has dyed her short hair jet black, all traces of the platinum blonde erased, my sexy friend looking downright amazing with the new color. Drea and Lyndsy are dressed as two of the tarts from Pamela Anderson Lee's television show V.I.P., and while I've never seen the show, the way both girls look makes me think it's time for some trash TV viewing.

I am dressed in casual Forties garb, and since I look physically as much like Ernest Hemingway as I do Ernest Borgnine, I carry a half empty flask of whiskey and a beaten up copy of *The Old Man and the Sea* as additional hints to my outfit. I also stained my fingers with a bit of ink, to add further to the whole feel of the hard working, tortured writer. We'll see if anyone gets it.

Drea, who seems to know half the people here, leads Lyndsy and I into the kitchen, which is lit up by dozens of candles and a few different carved pumpkins. Moving for the booze, I wonder how long it'll take before one of us, drunk and oblivious, catches on fire from one of the many burning candles. Hopefully, someone is dressed as a firefighter, or a paramedic.

At the very least, a mortician.

"What're you drinking?" Drea asks me loudly, trying to top the volume from all the partying and the sound system, which plays old Bauhaus in keeping with the night.

"Anything that requires an I.D," I say, and give her a nudge before adding, "Have I told you how great the hair looks?"

Drea smiles. "Yes, but you can tell me again."

I give her a grin and begin setting us up with vodka, knowing, one way or another, this Halloween night should be an interesting one.

TEN, MAYBE FIFTEEN minutes have passed and Drea, Lyndsy and I visit with Isaiah and his date, Talia, both of whom are dressed in full Blaxploitation garb and looking terrific. Talia is a "buyer" for Bloomingdale's—which when I hear this, reminds me of Chloe, and justifies a third vodka and cranberry—who Isaiah met when she came in for a little chiropractic care. Since then, Isaiah and Talia have spent several nights having dinner, seeing movies, going to hockey games, and just enjoying each other's company. I can see it in Isaiah's eyes, the way he pays attention to Talia, that he is very much into her. Seeing this makes me happy. I'm glad that my friend is sharing some quality time with what appears to be a quality girl. Drea and Lyndsy seem to approve too. Of course, buying clothes for Bloomingdale's must endear Talia to the girls even further.

On the stereo, Bauhaus has been replaced with some kind of spooky, erratic music that sounds a bit like the theme from the movie *Halloween*, which, given what day it is, kind of makes sense.

I glance at one of the four televisions mounted to the wall. *The Blair Witch Project* plays on it, it's volume either muted or drowned out by the combo of music and conversation.

So far, only a couple people have figured out who I'm dressed as, the copy of *The Old Man and the Sea* apparently going unnoticed for the most part.

The living room where we all yap and drink is growing crowded; our little group is huddled together like athletes going over the next play.

As Isaiah and I talk about the latest *Star Wars* stinker to come out, this girl dressed as Cat Woman begins to pass by. Both Isaiah and I are unable to keep ourselves from looking over the sleek, and wonderfully tight outfit. The girl stops and smiles at us, nodding in approval of Isaiah's *Shaft* costume.

"Who're you dressed as?" Cat Woman asks me, her tan face covered by an even darker mask.

I want to say something witty, but I'm too buzzed to concentrate. So I simply hold up my flask and copy of *The Old Man and the Sea*, and give this fine feline a smile, figuring the props will be enough of a hint.

"Aah, Ernest Hemingway! Very clever," Cat Woman says, the props having done their job. She then gives me this intense, sexy smile, her eyes lighting up as she adds, "You know what would've been really clever? If you dressed up as him *after* he shot himself. You could have put jelly and fake blood in your hair, walked around with a shot gun."

Mortified, I give her a weak smile, part of me wanting to soil my underwear. Cat Woman then says she likes my flask, gives Isaiah and I a "meow" and then heads off into the crowd, leaving us to wonder if she was: a) just fucking around, b) sadistic and insane, c) a budding serial killer, or d) all the above.

I opt for the last choice.

Isaiah and I look at our friends, none of whom have apparently heard any of this.

I turn to John Shaft and ask him to hold my hand, both of us scanning the room to see where the Cat slunk off to.

Isaiah then lets out a nervous laugh and shakes his head, mumbling, "That is one scary-ass pussy."

Amen, brother . . .

FIVE, TEN MINUTES later and the party is in full swing. Some guy dressed as a candy-striper comes by and passes out candy and sex-related treats. I end up with a Charm's Blow-Pop, a Tootsie Roll and two LifeStyles lubricated condoms. I pop the sucker into my mouth, and pass one of the condoms to Isaiah, telling him he's got a better chance of needing it tonight.

Drea and Lyndsy are being hit on by two knuckleheads dressed in togas (how original!). Drea's newly colored hair is still causing me to smile. She looks great.

I give the room a major scanning and start thinking about my screenplay, about how well the writing went last night. Eleven pages in one productive sitting. In the first real night of writing. Best of all, I'm happy with what I put on paper—for the most part. I think about doing a little writing tonight, after the party. Could be a good thing, not worrying about getting laid, instead working through the night on my script. Maybe I'll stay here another half hour and then quietly slip out. Maybe I'll pick up a four-pack of Guinness and pump out another ten, eleven pages.

I give the immediate area another look, noticing a few different cuties.

Maybe I'll have one more drink before I decide how this night should be spent . . .

"STEER CLEAR OF the White Rabbit," I say, flirting, to this girl dressed as Alice of *Alice In Wonderland*. It is a few minutes later, give or take a few minutes, and while my booze-induced-buzz remains strong, I am now edging away from plain old drunkeness (if that's an actual word), and therefore pouring myself another vodka.

Alice gives me a thin smile and walks away, my comment having had as much impact as if I had pulled out my schlong and slapped it against the kitchen counter. Then again, six inches isn't exactly "slapping" material.

Get out of here, McGuire. Go home and write . . . or at least, sleep.

"Hey there, Hemingway!"

I turn around to see Cat Woman standing beside me, a smile on her lips and a drink in her hand. And despite her freaky comment earlier, my eyes still go over her outfit (yes, again), her costume being one of my favorites of the night.

"Hey there, Mistress of the Morbid!" I say, her words about Hemingway's suicide replaying in my head.

"Moi? Never," Cat Woman says and gives me a knowing smile. Her eyes then focus on my face, specifically, my mouth. "Hey, you have a sucker!"

The Charm's Blow-Pop is half way gone. I take it from my mouth and look it over. "Some candy-striper with hairy legs gave it to me."

"Yeah, I saw him too. All he gave me and my friends were a bunch of Sweet-Tarts and French-Ticklers," she tells me.

"Sounds like you made out all right," I say and stick the Blow-Pop back into my mouth.

The music playing now sounds like Massive Attack, though it's hard to tell over the noise of the party.

"So what's your name?" Cat Woman asks me before sipping her drink.

"Terry."

"Huh. I have a cousin named Terry," she says.

"Never met him," I reply.

This must amuse her, because she gives me a smile and says, "Clever." Cat Woman adjusts her mask slightly and leans a little closer. "Were you going to offer me a taste of your sucker?"

We stare at each other for a moment, just a frisky cat and a dead writer, with some serious sexual tension brewing quickly.

I begin to grin like a fool, all kinds of thoughts flying through my brain. "Anyone ever tell you you're trouble?"

Cat Woman takes off her mask, revealing her face, her natural beauty. She then gently takes my Blow-Pop from me, dips it into her drink and pops it into her mouth, keeping her eyes on mine throughout.

Inside, I'm so fucking aroused I can't stand it. But the way life goes-mine, anyway—I don't want to assume too much, knowing the second I do, this moment will become nothing more than masturbation material for the next month . . . enhanced by Wesson, of course.

Still, I decide to take a chance and ask her if she's here with anyone in particular, as in "are you here with someone who wouldn't like this dance we're dancing?"

Cat Woman gives me this funny look and smiles. "You're cute, you know that?"

Standing here, with this sexy girl in a cat suit hitting on me, I decide that at least for the moment, yes, I am what some girls would define as cute.

A cheese head, but cute.

N
O
V
E
M
B
E
R

TEN

The Numbers Game

WHEN YOU'VE KNOWN SOMEONE FOR A LONG TIME, and have become used to certain traits and behaviors, it's unnerving to see that person thrown out of his or her normal state, to see them discombobulated.

Isaiah and I have breakfast in the Valley, the two of us munching on bacon, ham and eggs at Art's on Ventura Boulevard. For once, I am not the one doing all the talking. Instead, as my friend rambles on, I simply sit and listen, taking in what I can, going over what is really being said, and processing what is relevant.

Isaiah and I have been friends for close to five years. Good friends. Aside from Drea, there isn't another person in Los Angeles to whom I am closer. I would step in front of train for him, and I know he would do the same for me. Isaiah is, for the most part, a stable man; his career as a chiropractor is going well, and his personal life is usually doing even better. Half gentleman, half lothario, Isaiah is the kind of guy who—like me—enjoys women. He too, loves hanging out with them, talking, having sex, and being in their company, whether they are merely friends, or on more intimate terms. The main difference between us is that. I am typically a self-absorbed, neurotic mess, terrified by commitment, yet craving intimacy, where as Isaiah usually approaches things with a level head and a strong sense of reality. In other words, Isaiah thinks before he reacts.

This was not the case last night.

Apparently, while Isaiah and Talia—his girlfriend of the past few weeks—were in bed spooning and talking, somehow the subject of how many people each of them had slept with came up, dangerous ground to go near with any woman, unless you have the open-mindedness of Henry Miller.

After goading Talia for a few minutes, swearing numbers didn't mean a thing, Isaiah was able to get the answer he was looking for.

Just not the one he wanted.

"Twenty-nine guys!" he repeats a little louder than need be, causing a few of the old timers in Art's to glance over at us.

I give one elderly couple a slight wave, and look back at my friend. "You already said that. Almost that many times."

"Yeah, well, it's worth repeating!" Isaiah tells me, his eyes wide with frustration. "I wasn't prepared for such a high number. I was expecting something like, I don't know, twelve, maybe fifteen, guys. Twenty at the absolute most. The absolute most!"

"So she's been with a few more than that," I counter, popping a piece of bacon into my mouth.

"A few means three, four tops. Not *nine*!"

"And you lost it with her, huh?" I ask, then take a swig of my coffee.

Isaiah sighs, nods. "It was stupid. Talia saw my face, the way I reacted, and she got uncomfortable. And then I got out of bed, saying stupid stuff which I don't wanna repeat right now."

We sit there quietly, Isaiah reliving the moment in his head, me imagining it. Our waitress, an old lady in her seventies, warms up our coffees.

"I hurt her feelings, Terry," he says, his tone somber, his eyes on his plate of half eaten eggs. "Talia's a good woman, and I fucked up by tripping over what she said. But damn, twenty-nine guys . . ."

"You know what? You over reacted, that's all. Go talk to her and work it out."

Isaiah gives me a look, shrugs. "Yeah, I should. 'Cept, I have to admit, I'm not sure I wanna' keep seeing her now that I have this bit of information." He briefly pauses, then asks, "If you and Chloe were still together, and she admitted to having sex with almost thirty guys, wouldn't it bother you?"

Isaiah's question comes hard and fast, and the truth is, yes, that seems like a high number of men to be sharing the sheets with. And the thought of me being Chloe's twenty-ninth or thirtieth lover makes my stomach tighten.

"YOU GUYS ARE such hypocrites!" Drea blasts, "Twenty-nine, does not a whore make, sweetie. Poor Talia. What makes a person a whore is their attitude. If all you're doing is fucking anything that moves for the sake of just fucking, then yes, that's not cool. But who the hell are any of us to judge anyway?"

Standing in my living room, helping Drea hang a ceiling plant in the corner opposite the entrance, I realize I don't want to argue with my tough little friend about the current sex topic. Not only because she might hang *me* from the ceiling, but also because she's right. As horny young men—boys, we spend our single lives looking to rack up our conquests. I myself have slept with two-dozen girls, which seems like a fairly average number to me. But if my sister, or a girl I was dating admitted that she'd been with the same amount of guys, it would bother me. It's lame, I know, but the mindset is ingrained, and tough to relearn.

Not impossible, just difficult.

"You think Isaiah's bumped and grinded with any less?" Drea asks, looking up at me as I finishing screwing a large hook into the ceiling. "Pu-leeze. I love Isaiah, but he's as big a dog as any other guy."

Get ready, McGuire, you're next . . .

"Do you know how many girls he's slept with?" she asks me.

The idea of lying to Drea is so alien to me, but the idea of hanging Isaiah out any further is just as ugly an option. I already regret bringing up the subject in the first place. I look at Drea, at her pretty face, her curious eyes and shrug, saying, "I'm not sure."

"What about you? What's your body count at?" I toss back, suddenly wondering how many guys Chloe had slept with, or at least severely fucked around with.

I get off the step-stool, not wanting it kicked out from under me if my answer offends. I give Drea a look, searching her face for any hint of an ulterior motive.

"Calm down, sweetie. You tell me and I'll tell you," she says, trying to coax me in, which, of course, works.

"I'm not exactly sure, but I'm right around the twenty-five mark, give or take a couple. Probably a couple less than that," I say, hoping I don't sound like a man—whore myself. Then again, if Drea were Isaiah, or Scotty J, or even my pop, I would say twenty-five with pride.

Drea studies my face, a slight smile on her lips.

"I guess I would have to sit down and try and figure it out exactly, you know, before I gave my final answer," I say, and then add, "You know, draw up a list?"

A "Girls I've Fucked" list. How romantic . . .

"I have a list!" Drea boasts, her comment throwing me for a loop. "Yeah?"

"Yup. I keep it in this old diary I had when I was a little girl."

I look at her and smile, picturing Drea as a little girl, hair in pig-tails, chasing (or beating the hell out of) the boys around some swings, maybe the monkey-bars.

"I've had sex with twenty guys."

I look at her. The number doesn't provoke any major reaction out of me—thank God. To be honest, the way Drea talks so frankly about these matters of the bed, I halfway expected the number to be higher, which is strange, because being easy or a tramp is something I have never associated with Drea.

I shrug, and make a face. "Twenty, huh? Twenty is good."

"So, you'll still hang out with me in public?" Drea asks, teasing.

I lean toward her and say, with a grin on my face, "Long as you don't randomly grab at men's genitals."

Drea hands me the plant she brought over, and orders me up the step-stool.

TODD AND I are working together at Video Schmideo, the two of us tackling the arduous task of re-alphabetizing the entire Drama section. Stacks of both DVD's and videocassettes stand several feet high, their appearance resembling a big city skyline of looming buildings. As we go about it, I think about Isaiah and his current problem. I think about what he asked me, about if Chloe had had more sex than me, would it bother me? I think about my sister, Tricia, and wonder how many men she's slept with. Maybe Tricia is saving herself for marriage. Maybe she's decided to become a nun. I decide I shouldn't hold my breath on that last one, not with she and I sharing the same blood.

I think back to Las Vegas, when Scotty, Isaiah and I went out to Bessy's Chicken Ranch. How many men had that blonde cutie I talked to slept with? A hundred? More?

The bottom line is men as a gender are a bunch of insecure, untrusting fucks. From America to the Middle East. From Europe to Africa. Some men go so far as to have girls' vaginas sewn up to keep their women "pure," and to enhance the man's pleasure, so the jackass can feel like he's got a big schlong when they finally do have sex. And while that shit isn't commonplace here, we still wield our double-standard like some kind of sexual Light Saber, making any woman who speaks up or acts on her sexual impulses feel bad or guilty, as though she's in the wrong. We live in the most socially advanced country in the world, but we still act like we're living in the trees when it comes to equal opportunity debauchery.

Calm down, McGuire, you're gonna have a stroke . . .

As I work on the C's, I look over at Todd, who is busy with the O's. I glance around the store, which is fairly empty except for a couple in the Classics section.

"Todd?"

He turns around, looks at me.

"Can I ask you something?" I hope he's not offended at what I'm about to ask.

"Sure. What is it?"

I hedge for a moment, and then proceed cautiously. "Well, I know you're my boss, and this could get me into—"

"Don't worry about it," Todd cuts in. "Ask your question. Spit it out."

"How many people have you slept with?"

Todd's eyes light up at the question. "Thank God! Something to finally break up the monotony of this shit," he says gesturing with his thumb at our alphabetizing. He drops the two DVD's he was holding and a smile creeps across his mug. For a moment, Todd is silent. I can almost see the wheels turning inside his skull as he tabulates the numbers.

"Do you need a calculator?" I ask when another several seconds go by.

"Be nice," he says. Finally, "No, I've got it. Somewhere in the ballpark of sixty guys."

Sixty?!

I look at Todd, and while I am not gay, I am impressed. "And you find time to run a business when?"

"Oh, sixty's nothing!" Todd says, waving off my comment. "Believe me, I'm well below the average. In *that* department, anyway."

I look at him, my face apparently telling him all he needs to know.

"First of all, I'm almost forty. And don't forget that it's so much different with two men, than with a guy and a girl," Todd explains, then adds, "You straight boys have to work it for the pussy. Jumping through all those hoops for some action. It's a lot easier for two men to just hook up for the sex, without any of that other stuff getting in the way."

I sit there thinking about Isaiah and Talia, deciding that if Talia were a gay man, she'd probably be considered a virgin for only having slept with twenty-nine guys.

I stare at the shelves in front of me, at a half dozen DVD's of *Cocktail.*

"Why do you ask, Terry?"

I look at Todd and tell him about Isaiah's situation, about the way Isaiah freaked out, and how he now feels like an ass.

"He should!" Todd exclaims. "Does he like this girl?"

I nod.

"Then what's the problem? As long as she's not going behind his back, what's it his business who she got laid by before?"

"Well, that's a good question," I start, and then ask my friend slash boss another personal question, figuring we're already into the thick of it. "Have you ever slept with a girl?"

Todd glances around the store, making sure no one is eavesdropping. "Two. When I was in high school." Todd then makes this face and convulses a bit, trying to shake off the memory. "But I don't count them in my sixty."

"YO, TOUGH GUY!" I say the second Isaiah answers his telephone. "Get your black ass over here. Pronto!"

"What's up?"

"Have you figured out a way to patch things up with Talia?" I ask.

"I'm still not sure I—"

"Then shut up and get over here. Now!" I say, excited. "I've got something very interesting to show you. You're not going to believe it."

Isaiah's curiosity growing, he tells me he'll be over within twenty minutes, and that whatever it is, it'd better be good.

"It's better than good, my friend," I tell him. "Just hurry up! Oh, and bring some Wesson if you want."

Isaiah mutters something under his breath and hangs up on me.

"HAVE YOU TALKED to Scotty today?" I ask Isaiah as he walks through the doorway. He shakes his head no and I tell him to sit down on the couch. Once he's seated I turn on the TV and the VCR.

"What're we doing, my brother?" Isaiah is cranky, his mood no doubt the result of last night's events.

"Keep one hand free, and keep your eyes on the prize," I tell him.

On the TV screen is a scantily dressed girl in her mid-twenties, with too much lipstick and her long hair piled on top her head like Barbara Eden from *I Dream Of Genie*. A moment later this guy enters the frame, the guy naked except for his socks, and sporting a hardon the size of a Billy-Club. At the sight, the Genie girl's eyes light up. She mumbles something about their dates being in the next room.

"Terry? Why're you inviting me over to watch porn?" Isaiah asks, sounding edgy.

"We got a bunch of new tapes at Video Schmideo this afternoon," I begin. "And when I was putting 'em on the shelves I noticed this one's cover."

Now, as the blonde and Mr. Big Dick grope each other, a second blonde walks in, acting (barely) shocked that her date is with this other woman.

"And?" Isaiah asks me, impatient.

"And shut up and pay attention," I say. "See if you recognize anybody."

"Recognize anybody? What the fuck you—OH SHIT!" Isaiah yells as we watch Betsy, Scotty J's recent ex, moving toward the porn guy's monster schlong. "That's Betsy! That's *Scott's* Betsy!"

"That's right. One and the same. She's on the back cover of this porno we got," I explain. "When I saw her, I nearly shit my pants."

Betsy, the Genie blonde and the guy's appendage all begin to move with a certain amount of zeal, Betsy working her hips in world class fashion.

"You think Scott knows she's into pornography?" Isaiah asks, laughing heartily.

"C'mon. If he knew, he'd have told us." I say, half of me thoroughly amused and the other half feeling bad for the guy— Scotty J, not the dude in the video.

Isaiah laughs again, and claps his hands together. "Oh man, no wonder Betsy was giving him a bad time about coming too quick. The girl's used to coked-up fuck studs!"

I shake my head, picturing Scotty all bummed when we went running last month. "Poor bastard never had a chance."

"Should we call him?"

I look at Isaiah, wondering if we should call, not so much to bust his chops, but because he's our friend and he should know. Well, also to bust his chops.

"Would you want to know?" I ask Isaiah.

"Two days ago, I'd have said yes. Now, with Talia and her thirty men before me, I'm not so sure the truth is all it's cracked up to be."

Just as Betsy and her blonde counterpart are about to get worked from behind, I turn off the video. Isaiah looks at me like I'm half crazy.

"Speaking of Talia and her twenty-nine, think about how many cats Betsy here's been with?" I point out, hoping he'll begin to realize Talia isn't exactly China Blue.

"I know, I know," Isaiah says, throwing his hands up in frustration. "I'm an idiot."

"How old's Talia?" I ask him.

"Thirty-two. Why?"

I sit on the arm of the couch and ask him when, even if it's a guess, does he think Talia began having sex.

"I dunno for sure. Probably around seventeen or eighteen," he answers.

"Okay, let's say Talia lost her virginity when she was seventeen. That means she's been having sex for fifteen years. And she's been with twenty-nine guys, which means, Talia's averaging something like one point nine guys a year." I give him a look.

For a moment Isaiah just sits there, thinking. Finally, he quietly repeats, "One point nine guys a year . . ."

"That's just not that many guys, when you really think about it," I offer.

Isaiah stands abruptly, mumbling about what an asshole he is. He then gives me a nod and bolts for the door, saying he's going to go talk to Talia, and beg her forgiveness.

Once I'm sure he's gone for good, I turn back on the video, for, you know . . . for research.

A FEW HOURS later and I am deep into my writing, John Lee Hooker singing "Mr. Lucky" from my stereo. When I finish work on the latest scene, I take a much needed break to stretch and use the toilet.

I check my voice mail, the only call coming from Scotty J. He sounds tired, or high, and my brain goes over the video with his ex-girlfriend, as I listen to his annoyingly long message.

Scotty picks up on the third ring, again sounding strangely mellow.

"Scotty, it's Terry. What're you doing?"

"Hanging on the sofa, watching a movie," he says, slowly, and then adds, "Come on over. I got the bong out, and I picked up *Chicken Run* on DVD."

What is it about pot and cartoons? When I was in college, me and my buddies would "hot box" our dorm room, and watch endless hours of *Mighty Mouse*, *X-Men*, and *Underdog*.

I'm tempted to head over to Scotty's, but know that when the writing is going well, it's suicide to stop. That plus the fact, I wouldn't be able to keep quiet about Betsy being in one of the newer adult features at my video store. And to be honest, I'm still not sure telling Scotty will do anything but make him feel bad.

Then another aspect of the situation hits me, my brain going over *how many* guys Betsy may have banged just from her day job. The numbers could be staggering!

"Hey Scotty, did you and Betsy use any kind of protection?" The question pours from my mouth before I can edit.

Okay, you see that can of worms, McGuire? See how it's now "open"?

Scotty clears his throat and says yes, and then asks why I'm asking.

Having opened my big, fat mouth, I now have two seconds to either tell my stoned friend *why* his ex-girlfriend was great in bed, or work the bullshit like a madman.

I opt for the latter.

"Well . . .," I already sound like a schlub as I begin my spiel. "Remember me telling you about that hottie I had the one-night stand with on Halloween?"

"Sure," he says, then quickly asks if she gave me something.

"No, nothing like that . . . but that's what I was worried about, you know, 'cause we didn't use any rubbers or anything, and I was just thinking about it . . ."

"You're dick's not itchy, is it?" Scotty asks me.

I glance toward my crotch, and tell Scotty no, that my dick isn't itchy. The truth is, when Cat Woman and I went crazy, we each pulled out condoms, courtesy of the party's host being a thoughtful guy, who also happens to work at Aids Project L.A. I'm not thrilled about lying to Scotty about something that didn't even happen, but I decide I'd rather play the irresponsible non-rubber wearing friend than risk humiliating him with his ex's career status. Since they were safe, all telling him would do is throw him for a loop. Of course, this is Scotty J. He may see sleeping with a porn actress as some kind of cool, hip thing—like admitting to skydiving naked, or something more funky.

"Dude, you gotta always keep a rubber on you," Scotty says, the concern in his voice fairly touching. "There's too much shit you can catch out there. Know what I'm say'n?"

"You're right, I will." I agree, and then tell him to enjoy his chicken movie.

"I'm serious, Terry!" My high friend stresses to me. "Gotta keep one on you."

"I hear you, Scotty. I'll put a condom on right now, while I write. Just in case."

Scotty, oblivious, says "good," then laughs at something concerning a chicken . . . .

ELEVEN

Truth V. Praise

"EVERYTHING HAPPENS FOR A REASON." THIS IS one of my Grandma Kate's favorite sayings. And while at times I think it's nothing more than a silly old phrase, sometimes I wonder if there isn't some logic to it.

A case in point: my old neighbor moves out and in moves a single mother named Zoey. Zoey has a two year old boy, Simon, who is in the habit of throwing crying fits pretty much every night between Midnight and two a.m. At first I considered shopping for an infant sized muzzle, but then I decided that these specific hours would be better spent on my screenplay and "Single Schmuck" column. As a result, my column is done well ahead of schedule (a minor miracle), and my script's first draft is a few days away from being complete (a major miracle). I haven't done this much writing, with such a relaxed feel, in a very long time. Not since I was a punk kid, before Mom got sick.

So, if I were to buy into the Grandma Kate school of thinking, my new neighbor moving in was meant to facilitate my career as a writer.

And to remind me how not ready for children I am.

GIVEN THAT CHRISTMAS is less than three weeks away, Isaiah and I are out braving the crowds, trying to get through some shopping. I haven't been a fan of the "silly season" in a long time, in truth, not since my mom died. Yes, it's good to be with my pop and sis, but the holiday inevitably serves as a reminder that our nuclear family is no longer nuclear.

As mellow as I get around this time, the one thing that truly bugs me is the ritual known as holiday shopping. It's bad enough schlepping to the grocery store for Guinness and Macaroni n' Cheese, but to purposely head out during the busiest time of year and battle the masses for Christmas gifts, seems as nutty as being a kamikaze back in WWII.

Fortunately, Christmas shopping with Isaiah is a bit more colorful. After pit stops at Oliver Peoples on Sunset and Jerry's Head Shop on Vine, the two of us—Isaiah announces coolly—are headed for The Pleasure Chest on Santa Monica.

"Um, why are we going to The Pleasure Chest for Christmas gifts?" I ask, my association of these two things as murky as it was when Dennis Miller joined the Monday Night Football crew.

Here you go Uncle Dave, here's the tie you wanted, and those anal beads you've been craving . . .

"Come on, Terry. You sound like a prude," Isaiah says, as he makes a right onto Santa Monica Boulevard. "My cousin Byron and I give each other joke gifts each year."

"Joke gifts, huh?"

Isaiah gives me a look, "You gotta knock this Grinch shit off," he says. He goes on to explain how for the past several years, he and his cousin have kept getting nastier and nastier gifts for each other, ranging from "dribble" glasses to monster-sized dildos.

"At least you guys haven't forgotten the *true* meaning of Christmas," I say, flatly.

Isaiah gives me another look.

THE PLEASURE CHEST is filled with everything from vibrators the size of that midget in the *Austin Powers'* movie, to riding crops not quite meant for a horse's ass—though I'm sure you could use them there too.

While we shop, Isaiah and I talk about Talia, how she still isn't interested in getting back together. Isaiah says something about learning his lesson, and that he's going to buy Talia a dozen roses anyway, as a final apologetic gesture.

We also talk about Pilar, the lesbian filmmaker I met through Video Schmideo. In the last couple weeks, Pilar and I have hit Drea's coffee house a few times, the two of us yapping about writing and using each other to bounce ideas off. I suspect Pilar also likes seeing Drea, but that's beside the point. I tell Isaiah that as soon as I finish my script, Pilar and I are going to swap projects—she's also finishing up a screenplay—and critique each other's work.

While we browse the few dozen choices in condoms, Isaiah tells me for what has to be the tenth time in the past few weeks to get back in the game; that there are dozens, hell, *hundreds* of quality women out there who would love to hang with a budding writer who's on his way to big, big things. I remind him of my Halloween escapade, which he quickly dismisses with a wave of his hand, saying that doesn't count.

"Why doesn't it count?" I protest. "Because she was in a cat suit?"

"Because you didn't have to do anything," Isaiah says while looking over a twenty-pack of Trojan condoms. "That girl was gonna have you no matter what."

"No way, Isaiah! I could of—"

"Don't bullshit me, Terry. That Cat Woman wanted a one night stand and she chose you. Ain't no way you were getting outta that one!"

I consider arguing, but know Isaiah is speaking the truth. Since Chloe and I split, I had yet to pursue any real kind of sexual social life. Sure I had gawked at a few cuties here and there, not to mention finished off a bottle of veggie oil, but when it came to being available, I wasn't. I might feel a lot worse about this fact if it weren't for my current prolific writing streak.

Isaiah tosses the twenty-pack of condoms into his shopping basket, and says to me, "I'm getting these for you, so let it be. If you have 'em around, maybe they'll be an incentive to start getting back into the game."

I stare at the Mormon-sized pack, then mumble a thank you.

"You know, you should call Sabrina," Isaiah adds. "See what she's up to."

Actually, that would be nice, assuming she'd even be interested at this point. She did call not too long ago, and I do think about her. Beyond the sex, Sabrina was always fun to be around, not the slightest bit of relationship pressure ever evolving between us. At the very least, it'd be cool to re-kindle the "buddy" aspect of our old fuck-buddy arrangement.

Isaiah and I move along, my friend leading me into an area filled with frighteningly graphic Pocket Pussies. Without missing a beat, Isaiah picks one out and drops it into his basket.

Growing anxious, I decide against asking who it's for.

THOUGH ISAIAH HAS done eighty percent of the shopping today, he still insists on dragging me out for a drink, as an appreciation for keeping him company. We shove all our gifts into the trunk of his Passat, and then drive toward Lola's, the two of us yapping about the Lakers, and the current three game slump they're in.

Standing at the bar, Isaiah and I indulge in a couple green apple Martinis. It's good to be out of the shopping mode and having a drink, but the truth is I can't wait to head home and plow through some more of my screenplay. Though it's my first, I'm pretty confident with its structure and the flow of the story line. As far as serial killer type stories go, this one has a pretty unique feel. 'Course, I'm sure every schmuck who ever wrote a script thought the exact same thing.

"You hungry?" Isaiah asks, then sips his Martini.

"Eh, not really. You?"

"I'm thinking about some appetizers. You wanna share a plate of Calamari?"

I take a long sip off my drink and nod, "Why not. But let's not turn this into an all nighter. I want to hit the script pretty soon."

"Fair enough," Isaiah agrees, and then asks, "You come up with a title yet?"

I hold my hands up, in mock-pitch meeting fashion. "*Dead Dudes on Mulholland*. What do you think?"

"Catchy. Can you still get your name off the project?"

Isaiah and I finish off what will be the first of a few rounds, despite my need to head home soon. It's tough to say no to friends, and tougher to say no to friends *and* booze.

Just as we finish ordering our Calamari and another round of Martinis, two attractive brunettes approach us, each holding a Cosmopolitan and those tiny purses that hold lipstick, cash and little else. One of the girls, whose hair is in pig-tails, sloshes her drink as she stops in front of us, completely oblivious to her lack of grace.

"Hey," this girl says to me, her finger pointed closely at my face. "You look familiar to me. Are you an actor?"

Instantly, I feel Isaiah's eyes on me, as if to say, "Don't fuck this up."

I smile at both girls, my attention coming back to the cutie with the finger. "Me? No, I'm not—"

"Terry here's a writer!" Isaiah exclaims, clearly not trusting me to carry the ball.

Our second round of drinks is delivered, and Isaiah offers to buy both girls another round of cocktails, once their current supply runs dry. Given the fact that the one with the pig-tails and the live finger already seems tipsy, I question if his generosity is such a good idea, naturally keeping this thought to myself. When serving as a friend's wing man while meeting girls, it's a golden rule not to do or say anything to screw with the possibilities.

"You're a screenwriter?" The other girl asks, coming off much more coherent than her friend.

Yes, yes, yes! Don't belittle it, McGuire. Don't just—

"Not quite yet," I answer honestly. "I have a column. In *Angelino Style*."

"It's a sex column," Isaiah adds quickly. "Covers all the good stuff . . ."

I look at my friend, my expression trying to subtly convey that he should mellow out on the "literary pimp" approach.

Isaiah turns back to the girls and introduces himself, offering his hand.

The sober girl's name is Tyna, with a y not an i. The tipsy cutie is Jeanne. She sloshes her Cosmopolitan some more as she asks again who I am.

"Terry," I say, patient, now wanting a third drink. "Terry McGuire. Nice to—"

"Terry McGuire? Like Tom Cruise's name in that one movie, right?" Again, the finger is being pointed, Jeanne's manicured and Vamp colored nail dangerously close to my schnoz. If she draws blood, I'm not going to be happy.

"Actually, the movie you're thinking of is *Jerry Maguire*," I begin. "Jerry, not Terry. And his last name is spelled—"

In one nanosecond, Jeanne—the finger waving lush—slips into this unnerving, dark mode as she spews out, "I never saw that stupid movie, so, whatever!" She gives me a look that should, by all accounts, cause my head to explode like the victims in that movie *Scanners*, but, aside from wanting to shit my pants, all I feel is jarred.

For a couple seconds, I simply stare at this new millenium version of "Sybil," convinced that if I take my eyes off her, she'll break her glass and slice my throat wide open. She turns to her friend and says something I'm unable to make out. Both girls give Isaiah and I big phony smiles as they excuse themselves for the ladies' room.

"What the fuck did you say to her?" Isaiah asks, sounding confused and pissed.

"I don't know, but I'm not interested in hanging around to find out," I finish my Martini in two large swallows, hoping the booze doesn't inhibit my writing. "Let's cancel the food and get out of here."

Isaiah shakes his head at me. "You don't wanna stay? See if they come ba—"

I cut in, more than ready to go. "Yours may be worth waiting for. But mine? Uh-uh," I tell him. "I'd feel less anxious waiting for Squeaky Fromme."

THE COMPUTER IS warming up. The right music is playing. A bottle of Guinness and a bottle of water are in place. I am ready to write. I am ready to complete my first screenplay.

As I stand at the open front door, taping up my "am working—leave me alone" note, I hear someone coming up the stairs behind me.

"Hey cutie," Drea says as I turn around and see her.

"Drea Smith, what's going on?" I ask, hoping the answer is a short one. Not that I don't love hanging out with Drea, but I'm on the cusp of a writing milestone, and am fairly single-minded right now.

Drea spies the note on the door and gives me an unconvincing smile. "You know what, I only came by to say hey. Get on with your work. Give me a call when you take a break."

I know Drea's sincere about not wanting to interrupt, but her tone gives her away. Something has her down, gloomy.

Standing in the doorway, I ask her if she's all right. Drea tells me she's good, that she didn't land this commercial she thought she had in the bag. Two callbacks and a lot of positive reinforcement later, Drea would now start over, hitting another audition for another commercial, TV show or movie.

"I'm sorry, Drea," I say, wondering if there's more to this than she's saying.

Drea shrugs, and runs a hand through her hair. "You know what they say? 'You can die of encouragement in this town.'"

Moment of truth: I can tell Drea not to sweat it, that I'll call her later, and head for my desk, or I can ask her in, like a friend's suppose to do—in other words, do the right thing.

As opposed to the writing thing.

"Come on. Let's sit on my deck and share a cigarette," I say, offering my hand.

"No, babe. I'm gonna go," she says, her eyes darting between me and my sign.

I hold up my hand and extend it, again telling her to bring her "fine ass" inside. Finally, Drea gives me a genuine smile and accepts, taking my hand.

"I WANT TO move my career to the next level, you know?" Drea says, and takes a drag off her cigarette before adding, "It's been almost a year since I landed anything big. I've done some plays, but I'm starting to feel the money crunch. I'm getting nervous."

I look at her and nod in understanding. "Believe me, I hear you."

Drea takes a sip off the bottle of water we share, and another drag from her Marlboro. She leans her head back, blowing the smoke up toward the sky. "I don't wanna fail."

I watch her, my eyes on her face, on her short, black hair. I want to say something encouraging, but I also know the careers we've each chosen are tougher than hell to truly succeed at. I decide to try anyway. "Drea, whether it's my writing or your acting, the odds are against us. Truth is, we're supposed to fail."

Drea looks at me, says, "Hope this isn't your idea of making me feeling better."

I grin at her and nod. "There are thousands and thousands of people here doing the same thing. And every one of them wants to believe *they're* going to be the one who makes it. That they'll be the next big thing. And every day some of them head back home, or someplace else with their tail between their legs."

I take Drea's cigarette, and enjoy a long drag from it. Drea says nothing, her eyes back on the cool winter sky.

"But we're still here," I continue. "Just imagine, leaving L. A. and settling for something less than your dream. Always wondering if you quit too soon. If you gave up too easily."

"I'd never quit," Drea says quietly. "I can't even relate to that. It's not in me."

I pass back the cigarette to her. "And that's why you'll never fail! That's why you're one of the luckiest people in the world. You want to be a working actress—"

"Actor," she corrects, with a slight smile.

"—a working actor and you're out there every day busting your butt to make it happen. I mean, you've already had some serious successes. You've made good money doing what you love. We've both made money doing what we love! So many people out here never even reach that level. Were the lucky ones! You and me. How's that anything but a great thing?"

For a moment, we're both quiet. Next door, my neighbor's kid, Simon, squeals happily about something, his mom cheering and clapping with enthusiasm.

"You're right. I hate to sit here and moan about my life, but I guess I've let it all build up for too long. I need to vent more often." Drea turns to face me and smacks my leg. "You're unusually optimistic tonight. You either had sex or your writing's going well."

I inform her it's the latter, and invite her to hang out if she feels like it, while I work on my script.

"I'm gonna have one more cigarette and head out," Drea says, and adds, "You know, Terry? I know you'll hate hearing this, but listening to you tonight, you sounded a lot more like a man than a boy." Drea gives me a sly look and fires up another cigarette.

I look at her and playfully smack her thigh, "For God's sake, don't tell anybody. I don't want to have to kick your ass."

Drea grins and looks out into the night. We are both quiet, neither of us saying anything. Neither of us needing to.

WHEN I WAS eight years old, I discovered James Bond movies. I watched as many of them as the local TV stations would play, usually on ABC as their Sunday night feature. Lucky for me, mom and pop also liked 007, so they let me stay up and watch with them—as long as I headed for bed immediately after the movies ended.

At some point during my obsession with all things Bond, my mom brought home an old Signet copy of Ian Fleming's *On Her Majesty's Secret Service*. Though I was too young to understand a lot of what I read, the sixty cent paperback took me into a world that until then—book wise, that is—had been filled with slightly more youthful endeavors by Edward Gorey, Dr. Seuss and E.B. White. Watching James Bond on TV was one thing, but reading about him let my imagination run wild. My brain filled with endless images of adventure, danger and women (though for an eight year old boy, the kissing stuff wasn't very cool).

One day, I asked my mom if she thought I could write a story about James Bond. She told me to sit down and try, that she and my pop would read it when I was through. So with my copy of *On Her Majesty's Secret Service* beside me as a reference, I dreamed up my own secret agent scenario and wrote it down.

I remember handing over the story (in pencil, on that cheap

brownish-gray paper known as "scratch") to my folks, scared that they wouldn't like it. The twenty minutes they took to each read it felt like forever, half of me excited, half of me terrified. I can still picture the smile on my pop's face as he finished and passed it to my mom. Finally, as I sat on the floor near them, my folks looked at me, saying nothing, for what felt like a long time.

"Did you enjoy writing this story?" Mom finally asked me.

I said yes, and asked if they liked it.

My pop nodded and said he felt like he was there, like he and James Bond were in the castle together (my story had 007 sneaking into a mountainous castle in the snow, no doubt influenced by the novel I'd read).

"Terry, is writing something you would like to do more of?" my mom asked.

The "sure" I gave her must've been enough, because within a few days my mom had placed an old black Royal typewriter in my bedroom, a tablet of typing paper beside it. I remember the typewriter weighing a ton as I positioned it on my desk, and that it took me a while to master the hunt—and—peck technique.

Eventually, the 007 stories and Royal typewriter gave way to ghost stories (as a teenager I couldn't get enough of Stephen King) and a Smith Corona my folks helped me buy just a few months before my mom started getting sick. A couple weeks before mom died, I wrote her a story about a family that lived on an island where nobody ever got old, and everyone lived to be hundred as though they were only twenty. Mom kept the story beside her bed. I always wondered if she liked my stories because they were good, or if simply because they were mine. Either way, I liked writing them, and I liked writing some of them for her.

I SIT AT my desk reflecting on my childhood, at how unbelievably fast time has moved. I miss being a kid, punching away at the keys of my Royal, the unique sound it made. Computer keyboards lack that sound, that feel, of . . . accomplishment. Of course, the reality of accomplishment seems to come more easily and with less White-Out with a PC than it did through an old Royal.

I can feel myself getting more and more wired as I move closer to finishing my still untitled script. At worst, this draft will be done by tomorrow night. At best, tonight, probably while my neighbor's kid is crying.

It's weird, but the excitement and nervousness I feel as I come to this draft's completion isn't so different then the way I felt giving my folks that first story.

Time passes. Certain feelings don't.

My fingers work quickly, the screenwriting program matching my speed without any hesitance. I begin what is the first of my final three scenes, my hands slick with sweat from being so anxious. From being so excited. From being so hopeful.

Just don't let it suck . . . .

WHEN WRITERS GET together to help each other with their craft, one of a few things can happen. They will simply be honest, and all will benefit, their egos hopefully strong enough to withstand and process any legitimate criticism. Another possibility is that one of the writers will become defensive about anything less than a glowing review, and therefore feel the need to bash the shit out of the other's writing, even if they actually like it. A third scenario is that no one will saying anything constructive—good or bad—instead, remaining spineless and blowing smoke up each other's asses.

Two of those three situations happen all too often in Hollywood.

When Pilar brings her script into Video Schmideo, she gives me this big smile and tells me that she'll have my screenplay read within the next few days. I tell her the same about hers, and we both promise to be completely honest, because anything less would be typical Industry bullshit.

"Go ahead and make notes right on the pages," Pilar tells me. She then drags me down the aisle to help her find this specific documentary on the Stonewall riots.

As we look for her movie, I decide this is a good thing, two people sharing their work, not letting their vulnerability get the better of them. That this is all part of the process. That, as serious writers, the more you put the writing out there, the better your chances are something will happen.

Jesus, McGuire, you just referred to yourself as a "serious" writer.

Of course, if Pilar really trashes my screenplay, I'll probably charge fifty gay pornos to her store account . . .

IT'S A FEW days before Christmas and I'm working hard on a re-write, my mind on cleaning certain shit up, and little else. Once again I forget to turn off the ringer, so I pick-up when the telephone startles me. It's my pop wanting to tell me he's looking forward to having my sister and me around for the holiday.

"Well, we're both glad to be there," I tell him.

"Maybe you ought to bring that script of yours. Let me take a look at it," he says.

"There's no golf in it," I say, sarcastically. "Actually that's not true. One of my victims is killed with a five-iron."

On the other end my pop says nothing, though his breathing is audible.

"Dad, you there?" I ask.

After another couple seconds, he clears his throat and says, "You know, Terry. I'm sorry your mother's not here to be with us. That you and Tricia didn't have more time with her."

Thrown, it takes me a second to realize what pop is saying. I hedge at saying what I want to, then go for it anyway, asking, "Do you ever feel like we got cheated? All of us? About mom?"

When my pop does answer, I know he's fighting like hell not to get choked up, his words coming slowly, deliberately. But it's okay, because at least they are coming.

Fifteen more minutes go by, the two of us talking about all that has happened, and the way it has shaped each of us as individuals.

When we hang up, I realize that aside from my one crack about five-irons, we didn't talk about golf. Pop didn't mention it. No Tiger Woods, no handicaps. Nothing.

'Tis the season for miracles—however minor.

TWELVE

Schmuck, Revisited

"DO YOU HAVE ANY IDEA HOW HARD IT IS to follow an act like Jesus?" I yell at Drea, trying to outdo the loud music coming from the band on stage. The Opium Den is packed, the majority of the crowd here for the band playing, this trio called Lord Have Marcy.

It's a few days after Christmas, and one day after my Thirtieth birthday. Drea, Lyndsy, Scotty J, and I are here because Drea insisted on taking me out in honor of my big day. Isaiah and this new girl he's dating are supposed to show up—Isaiah's date also a chiropractor, this cutie he met while they were both at a convention in St. Louis.

"It is a big deal, Terry! You only turn thirty once," Drea says, our faces only a few inches apart. "I think it's nice, having your birthday in the middle of all these other holidays."

Lord Have Marcy kick into a cover of The Stones' "Gimme Shelter." Drea and I sip our Tanqueray Tonics, both of us grinning like fools as the crowd's energy goes up several notches. Looking at my friend, despite all the people around, I want to kiss her. I want to drag her off into a darkened corner, and tell her how great she is. How important she is, not just to me, but to everyone who knows her. Drea Smith is indeed that rare person that makes you a better person just by having her in your life. Not to mention she's incredibly cute, and has a terrific little body.

Apparently, Drea feels something too, because she leans in and gives me a kiss. And not just a peck, either, but a wonderfully long, warm smooch that makes me wanna take her home right now. When we pull our lips away, Drea and I stare at each other, the sexual tension brewing.

Brewing? Hell, the sexual tension is brewed and ready to serve . . .

Drea chews on the corner of her lower lip, a smile building on her face as we continue to zone on each other.

I can't take it any longer and laugh.

Drea gives me a slug in the arm. "What're you laughing for?"

I glance around at the crowd, at the band on stage, and then come back to Drea's face. "I was just thinking how good that was."

Drea smiles, and says, "Me too."

Hearing her use those specific words, I want to remind Drea that she's the one who said "me too" sounds a lot like "fuck you," but instead I finish my drink in one long swallow.

"Hey, Terry?" A hand grabs my shoulder and I turn around to see Scotty J. He tells Drea and me that Isaiah and his date are here. As the three of us move for our reserved table, Scotty also mentions that Isaiah's date has great, huge tits.

At the table, all six of us drink and yap. Isaiah's date—Sheila's her name—comes off as one giant sweetheart (and yes, Scotty was correct about her breasts). The more we drink, the louder we get, which is still a whisper compared to Lord Have Marcy, who are actually pretty damn good.

At some point during the night, one of the boys pulls out a few gifts for me and my thirty year old ass. The presents include two bottles of Wesson and a mini-basket of fresh strawberries.

Everyone's got to be clever.

Isaiah orders a round of tequila shots and upon their arrival, Drea waves her hands spastically to get our attention. "Wait! I wanna say something. Hold up your drinks!"

Lyndsy and Isaiah laugh at Drea, at her inebriated state. We all raise our shot glasses as my sexy drunk friend starts in.

"To my absolute favorite thirty year old neurotic writer friend!" Drea announces, and then continues, "You are everything a girl could want in a walking cliché. You're beautiful, funny, immature, sweet, confused, hilarious and beautiful—"

"Ya' already said beautiful," Scotty throws in.

"—and I adore you, Terry. Aw, hell, I love you!" Drea lays another kiss on me as though world peace were dependent on it.

Lyndsy, Scotty and Sheila scream and applaud in support, while Isaiah yells something that sounds like "It's about fucking time!"

Eventually, Drea and I come up for air and do our shots of tequila, followed with a suckle of lime each. Our eyes remain locked on each other the whole time.

While Drea and I make faces from the bitterness of our shots, this amazon-sized redhead bumps into our table and plops down onto Scotty's lap. The redhead then gives him a big, embarrassed grin. Scotty's face lights up as though he's just won the state lottery. He and the girl begin laughing, both of them carrying on as if old friends.

Scotty says something in the girl's ear, and she reaches across the table and shakes my hand. "Happy birthday!"

"Thanks," I say. I turn to Isaiah who shrugs, as if to say he doesn't know who she is either. Confused, drunk and horny, I look at this redhead, truly perplexed. "You and Scotty J know each other?"

Still on his lap, the redhead nods a yes and says they met over the Internet last summer.

Drea lets out a drunken laugh. Isaiah just shakes his head. I order us all another round of tequila.

Including one for Scotty's cyber-soul mate.

TWO HOURS LATER I lie in my tiny bed, buzzed, half-naked, and with company. That company being Drea. Drea, wearing only a wife-beater shirt and these funky little panties with Sylvester and Tweety-Bird on them, is smashed up against me, our mouths together, and our hands moving freely over each other. For the past twenty minutes (estimated drunk time) we've been fooling around in a way that makes me remember how hip it was to be a teenager, where anything sexual felt fresh and full of innocence.

Drea shifts a bit and rolls on top of me, "Terry?"

"Yeah?"

"I'm gonna tell you something, so don't interrupt me, 'kay?"

Before I can even answer her, Drea puts two fingers to my lips, her special way of saying stay the hell quiet.

"We're not going to sleep with each other tonight. I know you thought we probably would. Actually, I thought we would, but . . . but I don't want things to change between us. I can't afford to have things change between us, not in a bad way. And once two close friends screw, things always get . . . complicated. I want to be with you, sweetie. I do. I'm closer to you than any guy I've dated in a long time. But I don't want to lose what we've built. Do you understand?" Drea takes her fingers from my lips.

Though it's too dark to see Drea's face, I know her eyes are staring at mine. I know I'm supposed to say something here, but instead I simply pull her to me, giving her what I hope she finds to be a comforting squeeze.

I hear a knock at the front door, I think, but I still hold Drea against me. She kisses my neck and asks if I heard something.

"If you heard it too, I guess I did," I say, still not convinced. Besides, between lying with Drea and answering my door around four in the morning, I'll run with the former.

Then it happens: another knock, this one a little heavier.

"Should you get that?" Drea asks, a hint of uncertainty in her voice.

"I honestly don't know."

After a few seconds, I slide off my bed, and tell Drea to stay there. Only once I stand up do I realize how buzzed I still am, my equilibrium out of whack.

A third knock begins when I ask who it is. Isaiah's voice calls back, apologizing for the late hour, and that he needs a place to crash. Letting him in, it is painfully obvious he is also still drunk. I know no sober man would go out in public looking so haggard—even at this ungodly hour.

"You okay, tough guy?" I lead him into the kitchen and offer him a slug of water.

Accepting the non-alcoholic beverage, Isaiah goes on to say that when he and Sheila got back to his place, he noticed a framed picture of Sheila on top of his CD collection, a photo Sheila had put there herself. Apparently, Sheila wanted Isaiah to have a reminder of her once she was back in Cincinnati (where her work and life were), in case having eighteen-hundred miles between them made him forget how special she was. He then tells me how he responded to all this with a bit of trepidation (his words). Sheila then responded to his response with a bit of something called anger.

"She wigged," Isaiah says, taking his water and the pillow he brought into the living room. "She said if I was ashamed to keep a picture of her out in the open, then maybe she should leave. I tried to tell her putting a picture of herself in my place, without asking me, was like marking her territory or—"

"No, don't tell me that! You said 'marking her territory?'"

"Not like she's some damn dog!" Isaiah sits on the couch, and shakes his head. "I meant that it wasn't right to sneak that shit up there on me. She should've asked me first! Got my permission, you know?"

Both Isaiah and I sip our waters, while I wonder how many more seconds I should give him before I bolt for my bedroom. For Drea.

"So Sheila threw a major fit, all dramatic and shit. I think it was the tequila talking, 'cause she wouldn't stop," he continues. "And when she tried to leave, I told her no, that I would leave instead. It's not safe for her to be wandering 'round this late."

"You're a brave man. Leaving you're place in her care," I say.

"Yeah, well, glass and furniture can be replaced," Isaiah quips, unsuccessfully fighting off a yawn. "How come you're still up?"

"Because you knocked, genius," Drea tells him, now standing in the room's entrance, still only in her wife-beater and Warner Bros. Cartoon panties.

Isaiah stares at Drea, shock on his face. "Hey, girl . . . what're you—"

"Are you okay?" Drea asks, cutting him off from an obvious question.

"Yeah, I'm fine. Stressed, but fine."

"And Sheila's all right?" Drea adds. "You didn't say anything too lame, I hope."

"Nah, she's good," he says, then points at me. "According to smart-ass here, I compared her to a dog, but other than that . . ."

"Nice," Drea says. She then gives me a look before saying good night to Isaiah.

Isaiah waits until Drea's retired to the bedroom, then turns to me, grinning. "You son-of-a-bitch! Good for you, Terry," he says, and then adds, "Damn, she's got a great little butt! Did you see her butt?"

I lock the front door and shrug. "I got a glimpse."

Isaiah lays down on the couch, mumbling about needing a sofa for his office. I tell him where the aspirin is and move for the bedroom.

In my bedroom, Drea has lit an incense stick and a single candle. On the stereo is Sting, doing a cover of Hendrix's "Little Wing."

Drea says nothing to me, she simply takes my hands and the two of us do a little slow dance, with Indiana Jones and Kobe Bryant as witnesses. We move slowly, rhythmically to Sting's crooning, the song never sounding better. I kiss Drea's neck, and take in her scent, closing my eyes as I do.

Now this is one of those moments. One guy. One girl. Two friends. Two potential lovers, if I take it slow and respect her wishes to not push for anything more tonight. Of all the girls I've known, Drea is the closest to a perfect match for me. No matter how much we fight, we always forgive one another. No matter what is bothering us, we can always go to each other for advice, or simply for support. No matter what, we do what we have to, to keep our relationship working.

Drea squeezes the back of my neck affectionately, and kisses my shoulder. I open my eyes and glance at my little bed, wondering if she really is that put off by my bachelor décor.

"Now that you've actually been in my bed, does it really offend you? That it's so small?" I ask softly, figuring my charm has wooed her to feel differently.

Drea glances at the bed and then looks at me. "Speaking truthfully, as a *woman*, your bed is completely pathetic."

I stare at her, waiting for a teasing smile. It doesn't come.

Okay, so maybe charm isn't always enough . . .

WITH THE SUN up and one glass of orange juice already in my belly, I head for the front door to fetch the morning paper. I figure a few minutes of catching up on the day's events, another round of OJ, and then I'll take a shower, starting the day off right— on *my* terms. I pick up the *Times* and head back into my kitchen, my mind curious on the box scores of last night's NBA games. I set the paper on the counter and pour more juice, my eyes scanning over the front page, its headlines.

The main headline is about yet another possible conflict between the U.S. and some rinky-dink country somewhere in the Middle East. The next headline concerns local authorities arresting a woman in connection with the "Mulholland Murders." That late last night detectives questioned a twenty-something female after several leads and tips led them to her Hollywood apartment. The woman, a Chloe Saxon, was being held without bail and had—

Chloe Saxon? That can't be . . .

—refused to answer questions until she had her attorney present and was allowed a lengthy shower—

A shower? Chloe Saxon! MY CHLOE?

Somewhere, in the back of my brain, I comprehend that my glass of OJ has just shattered against the floor. I try and read another couple sentences, but am shaking too hard. Uncontrollably.

McGuire, you're probably alive right now because you "didn't" agree about Chloe's vagina smelling like strawberries!

I stare at the paper, at the words printed on it.

I wonder if this will make my script more marketable?

Standing in my kitchen, I want to giggle hysterically, with the emphasis on the "hysterical" part. I want to try and read on, digging up every morsel of info I can. I want to call Drea and Isaiah and everyone I know. I want another glass of juice and to crawl back into bed—hide under the sheets. But mostly, I want to shit myself . . .

Lucky for me, there's time for all the above.

ACKNOWLEDGMENTS

Nobody gets through the writing process alone, not with their sanity intact, anyway. I would like to thank the following people for their support and friendship, not to mention their endless patience with a certain pain in the butt . . .

Adam Barnes
W. G. Barnes
Jill Bushinsky
Big Don Crandall
Gisele Frazeur
Rich "Baby" Green & Dave Klein
Ann Marie LeMiere
R & R. LeMiere
The Los Angeles Lakers
Richie Patterson
The lovely Arlene Rettig
Jens Schmidt
The Weinstein Clan
Karen Woodward
and especially . . .
Kate "my better half" Luhr

www.ingramcontent.com/pod-product-compliance
Lightning Source LLC
Chambersburg PA
CBHW020334260626
47156CB00004B/1513